Contemporary Fireside Stories

An Anthology

Edited by

Philip Foday Yamba Thulla
&
Fatou Taqi

Sierra Leonean Writers Series

Contemporary Fireside Stories

An Anthology

Copyright © 2017 by
Philip F.Y. Thulla & Fatou Taqi
All rights reserved.

ISBN: 978-9988-869-78-6

Sierra Leonean Writers Series

120 Kissy Road, Freetown
42A Kofi Annan Avenue, Accra
Publisher: Prof. Osman Sankoh (Mallam O.)
publisher@sl-writers-series.org
www.sl-writers-series.org

This book is dedicated to members of the

Whatsapp Forum

Salone Writers Forum

Contents

i

Preface

Contemporary Fireside Stories is the second part of a collection of poems and short stories. The separate anthology of peoms, *Contemporary Fireside Poems* was published in 2016.

When the idea of a social media-sourced anthology was first proposed, it sounded hilarious to many, especially so when two seemingly inexperienced editors were similarly proposed, not knowing it could be a futuristic alternative to the 'fireside gathering' that was popular then. There was this frequently asked question among anthropologists: Does conversation change when people sit around a fire? The consensus was that, yes, it does change. Deborah Netburn (2016) states that there is value "in sitting around a campfire, listening to stories, singing songs and letting yourself stare mesmerized into the flickering flames…". This is not just a traditional African custom, but a typical Sierra Leonean avenue of 'edu-tainment', where cultures, mores and traditions are passed down by the elders, morals and lessons taught, whilst providing entertainment for the evenings before bedtime. Besides the entrenched belief that people are much more open when they sit around a fire, the expressed view, however, is that these public gatherings are no longer clearly visible among communities the world over. The communal medium has been eroded by the Internet or specifically, substituted by affordances that have closely paralleled the ancient fireside gathering.

The composition of this anthology, *Contemporary Fireside Stories,* is a manifestation of this dynamism and we are pleased to offer you this alternative. Stories published in this anthology share a common standard: writers sharing their thoughts via the Whatsapp forum, *Salone Writers Forum*, with contributions critiqued before being considered for submissions. In this way, social harmony and equality are promoted both with Sierra Leoneans in the diaspora and those at home. In a sense, the campfire story-telling and 'riddling' sessions are not altogether lost, and as Weissner (2014) *How Conversations Around Campfire Might Have Shaped Human Cognition and Culture* notes, has bonded the critics and writers (on the *Salone Writers Forum)*; helped them to share and entertain.

Th anthology, *Contemporary Fireside Stories,* provides a fine mixture of writers—there are 'old', expert, veteran voices as well as 'new', budding voices, and of stories with varied subjects and themes, ranging from historical, inward focused pieces on adoption and child-rearing experiences, sexual assault and its effects, travel accounts and stigmatization, romantic encounters, alcoholism, street life, sports, witchcraft and a host of other subjects. In a sense, this new crop of fiction blends personal experiences, social and cultural happenings with love that fashions some kind of bitter-sweet, happy-sad, swing as you read the stories. It equally blends multiple levels of narration each with their own unique style in a fascinating way to tell a story; mostly in the story-telling fashion.

The truth is, the anthology creates the space for a true and unique Sierra Leonean style of creativity, where spontaneity is not compromised.

In conclusion, we would like to express our gratitude to: Prof. Osman Sankoh (Mallam O.), publisher of the *Sierra Leonean Writers Series (SLWS)* for proposing this brilliant idea of using the *Salone Writers Forum* (a social media forum) as the source for the collection of this anthology and for recommending us as editors of the anthology; Gbanabom Hallowell for initiating the forum and bringing together Sierra Leoneans around the world who have a passion for the creative arts; Lango Deen Sesay, Kaday Mansaray and Abdulai

Walon-Jalloh for proofreading the final manuscript and making suggestions; and all members of the forum for their criticisms and recommendations. You are all highly appreciated.

PFYT &FT
Njala University / FBC, University of Sierra Leone

Bakar Mansaray

Running the Kilimanjaro

"Stacey to Steve and Lenana, can you hear me?"

"Yes, we can hear you. We're just about to arrive at the crater of Kilimanjaro," said Steve into the microphone of their two-way radio.

"How are you guys feeling? It's tough, isn't it?" Stacey enquired again, bringing her own two-way radio closer to her lips.

"It's really tough and windy, but it's an amazing sight," said Steve, a twenty-eight-year-old Aboriginal Canadian mountaineer and endurance runner. A line of cold sweat ran down his forehead onto the tip of his nose.

"And how about you, Lenana?" enquired Stacey.

"I can't find words to describe it. We're really fortunate to be here," said Lenana, a thirty-year-old Tanzanian.
He was another mountaineer and endurance runner whose sole passion since his teenage days was to run up and down mountains. Both leanly-built men were about six feet tall, and they stood strong like trees.

"Keep it up, guys. We're waiting for you here on Mweka Camp. Alex and Malcolm are saying hello. Over and out."

Not too long ago, on the day of her thirtieth birthday, Stacey Bachmann broke the existing women's world record for the fastest ascent on Mount Kilimanjaro.

Steve Mountain Horse, Lenana Kitali, a guide, and five porters were on their sixth and final day trek to Uhuru Peak; the summit of the Kilimanjaro, 5,895 meters high. It was one cool and misty morning in September 1973, and they had used the steepest, shortest and most direct Umbwe Route.

At the busy Barranco Camp, Steve and Lenana had spent a day acclimatizing for their upcoming race. One that would

2

see them running from Mweka Gate, the start point, to Uhuru Peak, and back. They had performed regular exercises to improve their muscle strengths, cardiac and respiratory functions. But they knew that such exercises could only help; they didn't necessarily guarantee good performance at altitude. They also understood that maximum exercise capacity decreases with increasing altitude. So, as they were just about to arrive at the crater of Mount Kilimanjaro, Stella Point, both runners thought they were ready to challenge each other. In the next few days, their physical and mental capacities would be tested.

Steve's goal was to break Lenana's fastest Mount Kilimanjaro ascent and descent record in a mind-blowing time of 6 hours, 23 minutes and 50 seconds. A first ever; worthy to be mentioned in the Guinness World Records. Lenana wouldn't mind breaking his own record or at least maintaining it. At stake was a gold medal and a cash prize for the winner, plus the exhilarating self-satisfying experience of running free on the 'roof of Africa' over rugged terrain.

At this point in time, Steve took a moment to reflect on his life and that of his late friend, Gaston Leduc. Gaston was a French Canadian; a mountaineer and an indomitable endurance runner. In 1970, while on Barafu Camp, about 4.5 kilometers to Uhuru Peak, 30 years old Gaston suffered from High Altitude Cerebral Edema. His brain tissue became swollen from fluid build-up in the cranium. Unable to descend quickly and seek medical attention, Gaston lost his life. That was a turning point for Steve who stepped in to fill the gap left by Gaston.

As if to add insult to injury, there was the nagging thought that couldn't be erased from Steve's mind; his recent divorce from Angelica—one from a child-less marriage that lasted for only nine months. Few weeks ago, he received a letter from the law court, through Angelica's lawyer, giving him an ultimatum for an overdue alimony. It was an issue that needed his urgent attention. Instantaneously, a warning-like voice inside his head said, *you better remain focused on your goal*. Indeed, Steve knew fully well it was what he should be doing now that he was less than a two-hour walk to Uhuru Peak.

"We're almost there, Steve," said Lenana, as the route became steeper towards the peak.

"Yes, time to take photographs and video footage," acknowledged Steve.

When the sign at the summit finally revealed itself from a distance, like Lenana, Steve couldn't resist that adrenaline boost to get closer. One step at a time and they were there. For them, the sign, a group of homey wooden planks, became a symbol of achievement. It read:

Congratulations! You are now at Uhuru Peak, Africa's highest point and the world's tallest free standing mountain.

But this was no place they could call home for long. The lack of sufficient oxygen and the cold was debilitating. So, briefly, they hugged each other, took photographs and admired the spellbound scenery; the wonders of nature in a place that was fondly referred to as 'Everyman's Everest'. Steve concluded that with resilience much could be achieved. Maybe, after the race with Lenana, he might draw attention to a worthy cause or charity.

Lenana felt inspired with a vision of starting a new beginning. His thoughts of creating a trust fund became overwhelming. It might be a way to help others by raising funds for some kind of awareness in communities within the Mount Kilimanjaro region.

Then, as if they heard a clarion call from the foothills, trekkers, guide, and porters did an about-face to Stella Point before continuing on to Mweka Camp.

Even though the impact on their knees from the seven hours descent was tiring and painful, yet Steve and Lenana had no need for trekking poles. There would be none during their upcoming race.

In the evening, once at Mweka Camp, they were welcomed by Stacey, Alex, and Malcolm. For a while, the threesome kept saying, '*Karibu!*' the Swahili word for 'welcome'. They too were mountaineers and endurance runners. Alex was white, a British from Brixton, London, and Malcolm was an African-American from Harlem, New York City.

"If you want, I've got some cookies and almond bars," said Stacey, as her olive-colored Zimbabwean face radiated a faint smile.

"An almond bar and some aspirin please and thanks," Steve requested.

"I'll have some cookies, please and thank you," said Lenana.

Stacey hesitated for a moment before asking Lenana.

"What do you think is the secret for a good team?"

"Good leadership," Lenana replied.

She gave him a satisfied look, nodding her head.

At nightfall, the stars came out, stunning nature into silence. But Steve couldn't sleep. He envisioned himself breaking Lenana's record. Worst of all, he could hear in his mind's ear the blood-stirring demands of Angelica, his ex-wife. It was only when dawn broke that he got any sleep.

He woke up later as birds broke into song. The other trekkers were up too. It was their last day of trekking. Steve stole out from the tent, ambled towards the forest and inhaled the sweet smell of the eucalyptus trees. He was greeted by a pair of malachite sunbirds perching on a protea flower. Nearby, a group of black and white colobus monkeys with spectacular tails were chattering; too shy to get any closer to him.

After taking breakfast, Steve, Lenana, and the rest of the team started the four hours descent from Mweka Camp to Mweka Gate. Steve began to wonder if his sore knees would carry him for the remaining distance of about nine kilometers. By mid-morning, it became hot and humid. Footpaths ran through dense vegetation and thick undergrowth that were populated by blue monkeys who were not worried about the trekkers.

On arrival at the Mweka Gate, Steve, Lenana, Stacey, Alex and Malcolm signed out with the authorities. Prior to giving tips in envelopes to their guide and porters, they were presented with summit certificates. By dusk, they were transported back to their hotel in Moshi Town.

Once in bed, it was Lenana's turn to reflect on his life. At the age of 15, driven by a desire to escape the poverty that plagued his unemployed parents, and coupled with an ambition to be successful in life, Lenana began earning money as a porter. While carrying loads of gear and equipment for climbers on Mount Kilimanjaro, especially foreign tourists, he improved his English-speaking skills tremendously. By the time he turned 21, Lenana stood tall and lanky, only to become a mountaineer and endurance runner with energetic strides. One bright day, Lenana competed with other runners in his first Mount Kilimanjaro ascent and descent race. He managed to keep up his strength for a strong top 10 finish. That inaugural race was enough to get him bewitched by the sport.

There was inside Lenana, like a defect in a jewel, a fear and apprehension of trouble with the issue of his two girlfriends, Chela and Abla. He thought of them with a shiver of uncertainty. Whenever he was overwhelmed by this thought, something would throb in his chest, like the breaking of his heart.

Chela was his main girlfriend who had been frustrated in her hunger for a husband. She threatened to abandon him if he didn't pay her bride price after the upcoming race. Her request came out in that distant, expressionless tone that terrified him. On the other hand, Abla wanted Lenana to pay her first semester fees at the University of Dar es Salaam. Earlier in their relationship, he had refused paying the fee for her Permanent Residence Application at the Canadian High Commission. So, as the day for the race approached, she had that anticipatory anxiety and dreaminess in her brown eyes that would appear and disperse like a mist.

On that cool Saturday morning, the day of the race, one of its officials introduced Steve and Lenana on the start line. With much fanfare, it was made clear to them that they would start at the Umbwe entrance gate to Kilimanjaro National Park at 1,661 meters, run up the Umbwe Route to Uhuru Peak at 5,895 meters and descend via the Mweka Route to the Mweka Gate. They were also reminded that no equipment, like homeopathic climbing kit, would be allowed. Both runners knew that it was going to be a mentally and physically demanding event requiring a high level of fitness and endurance. Dressed in long-sleeved lightweight fabrics, bandana for keeping the sweat out of their eyes, and sunglasses to block ultraviolet rays, Steve and Lenana were as ready as they'd ever be. They ran in Salomon Sense Ultra which were light and comfortable but without much grip on the sole. Both runners were then given the opportunity to do a television interview by Guinness World Records.

A cheer from the crowd greeted their departure. Stacey, Alex, and Malcolm were there to boost their morale. Once the gun went at 07:00 a.m., they had a few hundred meters of smooth running before a short and steep slope on the road. Steve held back until they got to the top then it was flat again, and Lenana took the lead. After about three kilometers, they left the road and started uphill on a narrow bush track. Steve was working hard and not letting Lenana pull away from him. After a while, Steve realized that he shouldn't have started that quick. He knew that in running at altitude, pace was everything. And going too fast would expose him to acute pulmonary edema. He started to have difficulties breathing which couldn't be compared to his performance at the same altitude during training. His legs and lungs were burning. Not being able to sustain the pace anymore, he had to let Lenana go with the hope of catching up with him later.

After a few arduous kilometers, Steve noticed that Lenana was also struggling to maintain his pace as the gradient got steeper. He was still behind Lenana and he knew that he too was tired. Both runners felt more burning sensation on their legs. As the cool morning gave way to the heat of the day, and the high tropical sun became intense, the runners reached more for their water bottles.

"Wait for me," Steve called out, as he struggled with his breathing.

"Are you joking? Run, man, run," Lenana said.

Steve picked up the pace and soon was side by side with Lenana. They ran together for about a kilometer.

"You don't need to be a champion twice," said Steve.

"Why not?" said Lenana, gasping for breath.

"Because you've to control your ego and…," Steve began to say before he felt like he was staggering; the trail went up and down. He saw the shadowed shape of Uhuru Peak but as they approached it, the trail went further. Then he felt like he was having the flu as his body, rocked by an irregular gait, became heavy and tired. Lenana whispered to him, hushed and in a serious tone, "The gods live here, so if you want to talk to them, now is the time."

As the two men were going in to the last kilometer they knew it would get steeper; it was going to be sheer hell. At this point, it was only their minds pushing them upwards; their bodies only followed reluctantly. From 1,661 meters they had reached almost 5,895 meters. They were breathing heavily and their hearts were thumping with effort. Unable to run upright any longer, both men crashed on their hands and knees breathlessly and they started crawling uphill. But just as they were about to reach Uhuru Peak, Lenana stood up, thrust his neck forward like a giraffe and took the lead again. He arrived at the peak one minute before Steve after running for 5 hours, 20 minutes and 25 seconds. He still needed to descend the mountain in less than one hour in order for him to break his own previous record of 6 hours, 23 minutes and 50 seconds. For one blissful moment, both runners spent about ten minutes relaxing. They ate energy bars and drank some water.

Suddenly, some beautiful slight flurries of glistening snow started falling. Only the reflection of the white snow and grey sky provided light. Although it made Uhuru Peak look magical, yet Steve and Lenana realized that it might well develop into a snow storm; one that could make it difficult if not impossible to follow a trail.

"Quick, let's go! The gods are annoyed!" shouted Lenana.

As if the gods heard his words, the snow started to fall heavily. The runners couldn't fend against the snow storm. They scrambled downhill in a spectacular descent, their feet crunched in the snow. The ground became slippery as they headed for safety via the Mweka Route of the mountain. In their haste, they bumped into each other and fell down.

"I'm sorry, Steve," said Lenana, struggling to get up.

"No problem. It's none of your fault," said Steve, as Lenana helped him to stand up.

In order not to fall down again, they bent their bodies slightly. With arms out to their sides to maintain balance, they walked flat-footed, keeping their center of gravity directly over their feet as much as possible. By watching where they were stepping and going slowly, they avoided the menace. However, the impact on their knees from the rapid descent became extremely tiring and painful. Once on drier ground, Steve and Lenana continued the race under the high tropical sun.

For the next couple of kilometers, they continued a steep descent, running side by side. Then, Lenana, the defending champion, picked up the pace and soon he had a one-minute lead over Steve. Lenana didn't look back. He made sure he ran every step on the slope. But each step was a struggle for both runners. They were beginning to get tired as they approached the foothills. The finish line didn't seem so far away. They ran through dense vegetation and thick undergrowth, interspersed with coffee and banana farms. The trail meandered through beautiful Jacaranda trees whose branches reached into the air and exploded into a riot of colorful flowers.

Lenana continued to have a one-minute lead over Steve. Suddenly, four blue monkeys stroke out of no-where like a bolt of lightning. They began to chase Steve and Lenana. The two runners slowed down their pace, trying to avoid direct eye contact with the monkeys. Next, they stopped running as the monkeys faked a lunge toward them.

"Hold out your open palms, like this," said Lenana, holding out his own open palms.

Steve did as he was told. He realized that in so doing, he was showing the monkeys that he wasn't carrying any food.

The animals looked at the runners in the eyes, opened their mouths, and bared their teeth. Then, they warned the men with grunts. Lenana stood his ground. Steve was about to continue the race; determined to break Lenana's fastest Mount Kilimanjaro ascent and descent record.

"Stay calm, Steve," said Lenana who picked up a stick from the ground and started shaking it at the monkeys. Steve found a stick too and did the same. Three of the monkeys retreated only for the biggest one to jump onto Steve's back. The monkey started drumming on Steve's head. Steve fought back; his disbelieving face looking like someone with a facial paralysis. Lenana struck the monkey on the head with his stick. The monkey abandoned the attack, disengaging itself from Steve, and ran away to join its troop. All Steve could say was, phew! The runners laughed their heads off for a while and continued with the race.

For a kilometer or two, they ran side by side. Then, Lenana picked up the pace and soon he had a thirty-second lead over Steve. It was at that moment that he started to have difficulties breathing. He felt a burning sensation on the back of his right hand. And there it was; a large blood-sucking tick. Immediately, Lenana stopped running but Steve didn't. He flew past Lenana, determined to break his record. The feeling of leading a big mountain race was enough to keep him smiling all the way to the finish line. Lenana shook his head in dismay at Steve's greed. He took a good look at the tick before gripping it closely to the skin with his fingernails and yanked it free. He ensured that the whole body, head and mouthparts of the parasite was removed without bursting it. By then, Steve had a two-minute lead over Lenana whose symptoms of discomfort rose dramatically. He started to feel really dreadful and wanted to quit the race. On the last lap, not being able to sustain the pace anymore, Lenana had to let

Steve go for the win. He diverted his thoughts to the vision of helping others raise funds for land degradation awareness in the Mount Kilimanjaro region.

Although Steve felt selfish, it was too hard for him to resist reaching the finish line at Mweka Gate in a startling one hour forty seconds. He broke Lenana's world record by two minutes in a round-trip of about fifty-three kilometers. For him, it was an incredible feeling to win. Then a voice inside his head said, *live in the moment and make the most of every single hour.* As the sun set and the temperature dropped to a pleasant coolness, he thought once more of drawing attention to a worthy cause in memory of his friend, Gaston Leduc.

Celia Thompson

My Brother's Confession

I must be blind with high resolution. But who will throw the first stone in an era where even the seers have cataract infested visions and prophecies are up for bids?

King was a man of few words although I had always noticed his gestures were louder than his words. To me, he was the loving brother who only needed to show up and dry my tears and he would always remain to be so. For a certainty, he was dawdling in his show of affection but had never brought it up for discussion and I never wanted to upset him. We had had many upsets in our family for as long as my memory could hold for any of us to stir a new one. We had had our fair share of singleness, abandonment and lack, which had made some comments better left unsaid. For the past 20 minutes, I had been watching King through my room window wrestling with Ras; again, a rare luxury coming from this man, whom I had loved and trusted all my life. Ras seemed to be taking advantage of this 'Christmas gift', and using all his energy to keep his uncle hooked to the game. I would have done the same, had I got the opportunity but there I was, sipping my tea with lemon, wishing I could trade places with Ras.

The 'playing' side of King was few and far between.
King was a 5 feet 8 inches tall man, with a broad torso that he had struggled to build over the years from lifting weights at our neighbour's house. The only house, which, if the rebels had asked for a wish list before they started the fire, I would have submitted its number without taking a second thought. Even its shade of red had irritated me. Sometimes, I wondered why King never took Ras with him when he regularly went to bench-press the weights, despite his

continuous protests. Ras could be a bother and sometimes it was difficult to keep him in one place. But could there be another reason? I knew exactly why I would never have wanted to see him go there, even if his life depended on it.

'Lod a Merci, mi sup!' A strong smell of burnt okra soup filled my nose, my throat and jerked me into the present. I sprang to save whatever was left of the soup, leaving my favourite tea cup in splinters. Oh no! I didn't doze off; I might have had one of those stupid flashbacks. "Why do I still have them?" It has been ten years now and I had had enough baths and scrubs to have washed the stain off my body. So, why was my body still tingling and shutting down when my mind pricked it? I had even done several Saunas and scrubs.

"Come in, the door is not locked".

I pushed the door open slowly and walked into an open space with a big bed in the middle. There were too many huge mirrors on either sides of the room and a clock on the right wall; the first thing that grabbed my attention, possibly it reminded me of the one we used to sing about in our nursery song: 'my grandfather's clock'. I had always wondered what it might look like and this one fascinated me.

"I hope you got everything, Please bring the bag to me. I have a back ache and cannot get up"
"I am sorry, Sir...very sorry," I stammered, "...very sorry.. The furniture in this room are so big," I ended, almost shouting.
"That's okay. I understand. You can look at them for as long as you want. You have always been my favourite girl in the neighbourhood"
"Yesss siiir...sss siiir," I grinned and then almost immediately froze to a touch. For a split second, I felt cold and I began to

shiver.

"Woo, I didn't know I had that effect on you." The voice was right behind me. My attention was fixed on the grand clock and I had thought as though a magical hand had come through the clock and touched me. I did not see Man leave the bed and walk toward me and neither did I expect him to. He had just told me he had a back ache and did not want to get up. *And what was he talking about him having an effect on me?*

"Man, what do you mean by that? I was very scared because I did not expect you out of the bed!"

Man, as if he didn't hear what I said, just breathed heavily on my neck and whispered,

"I have loved you since the first day I saw you; when we moved into the neighbourhood".

What is all this nonsense he is talking about? Is he so sick that he has become delirious? I thought but I did remember when he and his family had moved to this house five years ago. Then, I was only 10. He always had seemed a nice and caring young man who had a listening ear for everyone and a gift at the right time. I did remember one hot afternoon when he had appeared right in time at our house to save me from the wrath of my mother's cane after I lost the last money we had for food.

God be my witness, I still could not understand how the money had disappeared but I remembered that, on my way to the market, I had stopped to watch a small crowd of people playing lucky cards. The manner in which the man was switching the cards and saying, "...take this, you win; take this, you lose" was quite intriguing for me, until after that day when I vowed not to ever bat an eyelid whenever I passed by them.

Man had later told me, he had heard the loud interrogations from my frustrated mother and my pitiful responses; and had suspected I was in trouble. He had freely come through the yard, walked to the back where our kitchen was and to the spot I was being interrogated. Thankfully, he was able to calm my mother, putting smiles back to our faces. He had dipped into his trouser pocket and taken out some new notes which he had handed over to my mother. "Madame, please use this for the food," he had said with a smile and then hastily left. If Man had already received a 3-star award in our house, he would possibly have received a 4-star on that day, for I was sure my skin would still have carried the marks, if the General had not walked in, in the nick of time. So he wasn't lying when he said that I had always been his special girl. He had always looked at me in a tenderly way, even softer than that of King's. Looks that had made me wish sometimes he was also my brother.

At another time, I was at the communal street tap fetching water when the tap in our compound was disconnected because of some leaking pipes. When it was my turn to fill my bucket, an older girl stepped in and pushed me aside wanting to take my turn. I saw her raise her hand to slap me as I tried to resist her. Then, suddenly, I saw a bigger hand seize hers in mid air. I turned to see who this saviour was, and there he stood, Man! I was very pleased that he had saved my face and my pride because I was going to be given a good beating to the pleasure of the other girls who always enjoyed such street fights. However, on that particular night, I wondered if Man was my guiding angel because he seemed to have the sixth sense to know whenever I was in trouble and where ever I was. "Perhaps he keeps following me," I had whispered.

That was how our friendship welded over the years and I would come to their house and go freely. Man was 15 years my senior, and I thought it was strange that he didn't have a girlfriend. He had a good job as a banker and practically lived alone in their big house; unless when his parents and siblings came home on holidays from Europe. Since he lived alone, I had practically done his domestic errands, especially on weekends. It was a joy for me to help this man, whom I had come to see as my 'guiding angel'. And that was exactly what I was doing that day. I pretended not to have heard his confession of love for me because he was not only sounding different to me, but standing too close to my skin, which was making me very uncomfortable. I had been reading a lot of *Mills and Boon* romance novels and had perfectly read of scenes as the one I seemed to be in at that time. But all too soon and before I could take the advice of the warning sound ringing in my head and move a muscle to leave the room, Man had put his hand around my hips and lifted me from the ground.

"Let me go," I protested, trying to kick against the body of this man that felt like rock.

"Do you know how long I have waited for this, O!" he said softly, almost to himself.

"I have noticed how the boys in the area look at you and I am not going to let them harvest what I have watered. You are mine" and with bated breath, he lifted me off the floor.

"I am going to shout," I said in a defiant voice, choking on my words as I could no longer control the sobs in my eyes and the bile was popping into my throat. "Am not yours! You are my eldest brother," I screamed.

"I am not your brother! Shout all you want....you are mine!" he shouted hysterically.

So this was it. The gifts, the heroic acts, the smiles... Man, my saviour would become my terrorist. The man, whom on most days, I had preferred to my own brother, was here trying to take my pride. He plucked my breast from my bra and started eating it as a vampire would.

"You are so fresh and ripe....HMMMM....for me.... only for me," he muttered hungrily.

So it was true; there is no free lunch. Who is going to save me now? The man who has been saving me, has captured me, I thought and fought even harder. Man was stripping me off my clothes as an angry monkey would do to a banana. Ferociously! He was lying on top of me and I could hardly breathe. Still sobbing, I continued to wriggle and plead with him, "Please, don't do this to me. I am only 16. Or...or...maybe, you can marry me so that I become your wife, you can marry me...." but Man just laughed to my face and without a word, tore my flesh. He took my virginity; he took my pride. The pain Man inflicted on my body was less severe than the one I felt in my heart. He killed my dream; a dream I had lived for and had enjoyed every night. The only secret and price I was working toward. I had always dreamed of the day I would meet my husband: Entering the chamber from the bathroom, sweetly perfumed with Persian spices, I would linger at the door to heighten my husband's excitement. Dressed in lace *nightie* embroidered with my husband's name, I would walk majestically toward him, fully confident of my value and how proud I was going to make him. Reaching the bed, I would kneel down before my husband and wait for him to lift me up to him. Then, in confidence, I would surrender myself; a pure sacrifice. This was the only gift I was going to take with me; pure and fresh, to be tapped by my husband; my husband only!

19

As Man raised himself from my torn flesh and crushed heart, I picked up my clothes to cover my cursed body. It was no longer pure for sacrifice and the dream had been destroyed. I knew, from now on, I would only have nightmares.

"Why are you still crying? You were going to do it sooner or later and you should be happy that it was with someone like me," he boasted from where he lay, sounding satisfied.

"Take the money on the table, it's for you," he scoffed. As he said so, I rushed out half naked. This humiliation was too much. Not only had he defiled my sacrifice, pierced my heart and dirtied my body, but he had the effrontery to gloat about it and now he was paying me.

It occurred to me:

THIS WAS MAN
I WAS A WOMAN

He had never seen a sister in me. But where did I ever get that stupid idea from? King had told me once that I was stupid and I believed him now.

"King! King! *Di sup don Bon o*. Of all days, I chose to burn your favourite soup". If you wanted to keep King longer by your side, you should give him Okra. He said it was quicker for him to eat and the iron, good for his bones.

"This is why you should get married so that your wife will take her time to prepare your food," I mocked him. "The girls don't like me," he shouted back at me, catching his breath as he jumped up the goal post to catch the ball Ras had shot at him. This had been his automated response for years now. He knew as much as I that he was lying. If it was about personal beauty, King had it. He also had money to spend. I had seen a number of girls come and go from time to time but none had lasted a year. Before our father left the house to live with his girlfriend, he encouraged him to find one girl and be serious. But who was he to give such an advice? He was hardly home. He had more clothes than money. He was only home when broke and had lost face to his creditors. Once, one of his female creditors came to collect her money at 5 am. Luckily, he was not home that morning because he had not returned the previous day. My mother patiently listened to the stories that the lady told, one after the other, and after she left, my mother told me that the lady sounded more like a forsaken girlfriend than a common creditor. When my father returned in the afternoon; the neighbours were entertained. That was the kind of father we had, King and I.

King, upon hearing that the soup was burnt, ended his game with Ras and came through the back door to the kitchen. King loved his food. He went straight to the stove and opened the pot to check if it was still eatable. I made a face at him and Ras bellied out a provocative chuckle and sped past us, running back into the yard.

"Was he laughing at me?" King enquired.

"I think he was laughing at something very funny," I replied scornfully. Strangely, King did not laugh. Instead, he turned to me and with a very confusing look, which made me coil inside, said slowly and calmly, "This has got to stop."

"Then get a wife. After all, I am not your cook so if you don't want your food burnt, go and pay the pride price, and then get a wife".

"Fancy, this has got to stop; your mind is killing your body". King was dead serious. If he called me by my name, then he wanted to talk. On all other occasion, I was 'Sis'. "I am sorry I burnt the soup. I have a headache and should have slept a little longer this morning," I said apologetically.

"Fancy, for the love of God ...STOP IT..." He looked into my teary eyes and lowered his voice.

"It's gone ON for too long and I think we need to talk and now..." he said in a matter-of-fact way, mumbled and then put a hand on my shoulder.

"I know you were having one of those dark flashbacks. You will never change what happened. Move on!" he said persuasively.

"Fake smiles don't heal ulcers; they are only plasters that inflame." He stopped and gazed blankly into the air.

"I lost my innocence long before you did," King said slowly and painfully.

"My voice broke, my boyhood was botched, not a word," he sneered.

"In fact, I was assured it was the normal life for a man, whiles you were scorned and scorched."

No...No...No. This is not King. Some spirit has possessed my brother, I thought. He held my hand and slowly led me to the chair behind the door; my mother's favourite spot of the Kitchen, where she sat on the day Man saved me from her wrath. As if in a trance, I followed King and sat down. He brought in a bench and sat in front of me.

"Fancy, I know Man raped you almost ten years ago. I don't know why you chose to bear the humiliation alone and I respect your decision".

I opened my mouth to say something, and he stopped me.

"Shhhhhhh! Let me talk. I was also raped in that same house. I tried to warn you in many ways that things were not as they seemed to your innocent and all-believing eyes and mind. But you, my little Sister, were too green to read the different shades of yellow and red. And I, your brother, had been initiated into a party that tied my tongue. I failed to protect you.

And then, on that day, our mother found out that you were pregnant, I felt suicidal. I can still hear Mama heaping curses on you, saying that you were a useless girl and good for nothing".

With these words, I attempted to speak but I couldn't utter more than the syllable, 'I' and then buried my head in my hands.

"Do you remember that day when I was so angry with you and I told you that you were stupid?" I nodded. By now, I had lost my ability to voice my emotions and I could feel my blood draining from my head. I felt dizzy and had to hold on to the bench King was sitting on. This was another 'Christmas gift' and I had to make the most out of it.

"It was after I realized that you were only a prey for Man and he was going to eat you on the day he chose. Unfortunately, I did not know how to warn you. Our family was already scattered even before Daddy left and I was shattered as a little boy. I was raped at 14 and by 15; I was already recruiting other innocent souls that were defiled during those monthly loud parties. I dined with the devil on the same table as you did," he exposed and continued with teary eyes. "Except that you lost your confidence and I, gained a dirty confidence under the blind watch of our parents. I grew taller, perfecting my dirty act, not a word of concern from our parents. Those nice lunches that we had with Man at this house were the leftover of the soiled meals from the previous day. They had come in their best cars, dressed to kill, wearing perfumes that smelt out of this world. With such affluence, who would question the generosity of these men? Your own brother walked on top of you to pay them allegiance. Every time I saw your tear-stained eyes, I inwardly cried with you but was suppressed in my revolt. Where you exhibited your tears, I gained favour from society. I grew longer and tougher, filed in, not a word from our parents." Tears were now draining from his eyes.

"I dreamt about the best, our university graduation ceremonies and your wedding; where I will give you off to the man of your choice. Oh Fancy," he rubbed his hands on his head; his eyes were red as fire.

"I wanted the best for us; I wanted the best for our mother. I wanted to make our father regret all the poor decisions he made. Who should I have told? Where was father? Mother was going through a deep psychologically pain which she tried to manage well. Man was paying my fees and was good to everyone in the family. We had nothing. We had no one. So, he posed as our Saviour and while we looked onto him for mercy, he marred us. I think that I am as mad as you are, with a desecrated mind," cried, my brother.

"Except that unlike you, I lack the strength to pin the cocoon and dissolve this Utopia. All these years, I have not been able to fight the demons within me; for I fear to escape this labyrinth for the abyss," confessed, my brother.

'Look at me, look at me' I heard. *But I don't want to be here let alone look at these giants in the room*, I thought. I might have fainted and been slipping in and out of consciousness because when I finally opened my eyes, with a throbbing headache, I was lying on a hospital bed and Ras was sitting next to my head with his head on my bed, sleeping, his one hand entangled in one of mine. Ras did not deserve what was happening to him and this young man had had too much to process in one day.

24

"She is awake", I heard King say excitedly. I turned in the direction of his voice and saw a nurse standing next to him. They both quickly came to my bed and the nurse asked me how I was feeling. She told me that some tests had been done and she was going to check if the results were ready. As soon as she closed the door, King knelt down by my bedside, took my other hand in his and said, "Fancy, help me. I am dying."

"I am the one dying here, right," I scoffed. He opened his mouth to say something but then closed it slowly. He closed his eyes for some seconds and when he opened them, they were blank. He looked into my eyes and beyond as if he was looking for some answers. We stared at each other for some minutes without a word. We didn't need them. I felt his grip loosening on my hand and I panicked. I quickly found my voice.

"I am sorry. I have no right to judge you. Who am I to?"
He still did not say anything but this time he smiled. A very pure and selfless smile; one I didn't know he had the ability to offer. Don't know whether it was the purity or selflessness in the smile that triggered my soul and pumped adrenalin into my body. But I quickly yanked my upper body to try to sit up and disentangle my hands from both King and Ras; the latter who had been quietly engaged in everything and was trying to make sense of it.

"Let us go home," I said, "I need to find my brother!"

Fatou Taqi

A Complex Situation

"My ohhh my, you are pretty", he had often said. I'd heard this and similar flattery so many times coming from his room, where at different times, I recalled meeting different shades and hues of women and girls being entertained. I had always wondered what antics he was up to and had remembered feeling sad and angry with the 'victim' at the same time. How could it have been possible for these girls and women to be so shortsighted and idiotic? How could they not have suspected that he was a 'player' when he declared the same thing to each and every one of them? I also fondly recollected him coming out of his bedroom to meet me in the kitchen. "Namsy, I am really, really hungry. What can you conjure up for me…emmm, I mean us?" We had gone through this ritual every time that I was in the kitchen. From my little experience, I had advised that he needed to settle down; have ONE girlfriend who he could later marry because something had told me that he could DEFINITELY not continue in that manner without having grave problems, if not sooner, later. I guess, with me being younger and a girl, he had obviously thought that I would not have much to say to him in terms of giving advice. His normal retort had always been, "NOTHING will go wrong! What do you know, anyway, that I do not know already?" With those words, I had developed the propensity to 'brace' myself for the 'trouble', for when it would come and the moment when I would say, 'I told you so!' So my response had always been to give him my signatory Cheshire cat grin and change the subject, "Something edible will be ready soon for you. I promise." He would always finish the conversation with his customary final statement "That's my girl. I'm impatiently waiting".

Alpha was my older brother whom I lived with at his two-bedroom flat, just off the university campus on Mill Road. He was a public worker who walked in the corridors of power and decision makers. This had led him to affluence, of the nature that we had not really understood. Even though Alpha was older and actually took care of me as my guardian, he was quite 'simple' and I could hardly trust him to make proper decisions by himself or even on my behalf. As the older one, he became my guardian by default as our parents were very old and had refused to move to the city. They were both uneducated and had raised us through their humble profession as farmers. With their meagre funds, we were sent to basic school and after Alpha completed his O' Levels, he moved to the city, Freetown, to seek greener pastures. Because of his excellent results, he was identified by some 'well-wishers' whom I had teasingly referred to as his 'godfathers' to be enrolled at an institution where public workers, decision makers and law makers were trained. This premier institution had produced most of the leaders in the country because they were earmarked to be 'leaders' in the different spheres of governance. It was notable and notorious in being the breeding ground for future politicians (depending on the lens one wears). He was on full scholarship at the institution and enjoyed the posh facilities of the high expectations of the public worker lifestyle. What was ironical was the fact that it was an institution for religious and moral uprightness. In fact, that was where the complex situation conceived itself.

This institution, now nicknamed the 'School for Rogues' had earned that name because it was seen to propagate; doing all the things that the religious books warn us against. It gained on the theme of prosperity and 'get rich quick or die trying' philosophy. The motto, as well, spoke volumes, 'No alternatives, no middle ground, no surrender' and therefore the institution was strictly residential, so that there were no external influences to water down or question the philosophy. Alpha initially was a misfit within the institution because anytime he wanted to do as proposed, he had had bouts of imagining, seeing our parents who had taught him otherwise. He was therefore always in trouble but the head of the institution, Prof Dr Alakhi, had strong faith that they would succeed in making him their star student. At the school dormitories, Alpha, at times, would wake up with a start and shout out, "I cannot, I will not". His roommate, Jacob, became very suspicious that Alpha was not 'normal'. "Who would not want to get so rich, so soon? What is wrong with this man? Why does he not want the enormous houses and posh luxury cars that he sees the professors and public workers with? Does he realize that they were the chosen few?" Such were the questions pricking his mind. In fact, because of the mix of well-educated and almost downright near illiterates within the 'chosen few' circle, it had become 'normal' to see the two sides scurrying to siphon the limited resources available for the entire populace for their own personal use and bragging about who could outsmart the other faster and more aggressively.

Alpha, as envisioned, conformed and excelled in all subjects and all aspects of his stay at the institution beyond expectations. He became a star student and was constantly awarded with gifts and prizes for all facets of the sojourn at the school. He became the favorite of some of the tutors and specially the head, the Professor Dr. After three years at the institution, Alpha had been well groomed and was ready to take a place in the citadel of public service and governance. Alpha fitted in very well, and immediately started making strides to practise what he had been taught and what he had learnt at the 'School for Rogues'. Within a few months of graduation and starting work, Alpha had acquired two luxury cars and was constructing two mansions simultaneously in a very affluent area of town, with a long string of girlfriends to quench his manly wants. He was seen as very successful and admired whilst other people saw him as a stooge, a thief and a highly deceitful individual. Of course, that did not matter to him as he was making himself proud and making his alma mater proud too. "What does it matter what other people think? They are either very jealous of me and my quick affluence and want what I have or they are non-entities, whose opinions don't matter". These were thoughts that sometimes crossed his mind when he realized that there was also chronic poverty around him, especially with true and honest people. Besides the extravagant life, Alpha had led a fully immoral life. With as many as he could not count girlfriends, he had seen himself as fulfilling his duty as a man especially, as an alumnus of the 'School for Rogues'. "I am very liberal and understanding," he had habitually told his mates. "I create equal opportunities and I fully respect diversity. Regardless of the age, size, height, skin tone, intelligence, social class etc, I DON' T DISCRIMINATE!" he had vehemently declared so many times.

One fateful morning, Alpha had woken up at around 5am, feeling very drained and tired. He had had a terrible dream and was very confused. "Why don't I feel right? Why do I have this restless feeling?" He couldn't understand neither could he shake the feeling off. It looked like it was the start of his worst nightmare. At work that morning, whilst busy negotiating a lucrative deal, he had been told that he had visitors. They were two female police officers from the Family Support Unit Headquarters. After the usual pleasantries, the female officers respectfully told him that there was a complaint from a parent, who was claiming that Alpha had deflowered their fourteen year old daughter. "How can that happen?" he had asked himself. But a small voice in his mind reminded him of his previous utterances, "I do not discriminate". Ha! *How can this catch up with him?* It turned out that the girl had been HIV positive since birth and her parents had been very watchful and guarded their daughter very well. A picture of Sally was shown to him and Alpha recalled forcing himself on her, even though she had resisted. It was at a sports-exhibition at the national sports grounds and he had had more than his normal intake of beer. She had looked much more mature and older than fourteen, and he correctly recollected the round, succulent breasts that he had hungrily sucked and bitten. Fighting her, he had prodded everywhere and all over her, using his hands, toes, lips, tongue and whatever part of his anatomy he could use. He vividly remembered that when he had overcome her and pinned her down against his car, he was quite surprised that she was still a girl, still a virgin, still fresh and untouched, very tight, even quite painful—so much so that his manhood had been left bruised all over after the assault. Boy, had he enjoyed it? He enjoyed the battle and the struggle, he enjoyed the thrills and throes of forcing himself on her, and now, now…he was being questioned for underage sex, being accused of rape and to top it up, being likely diagnosed to have contracted HIV. Thinking about all these likelihoods now, Alpha realized that he could neither even remember her name, nor had he made any effort to even be 'nice' to her, fully aware that he had taken her innocence from her. Alpha was in a daze and his thoughts drifted back to his boyhood days. *What did my parents teach me?* There was a lot of emphasis on honesty, good morals, do not cheat, do not tell lies, do not steal or take something that is not yours, be polite, be respectful, respect women, don't accept bribes etc. etc. etc…the list went on and on and on. No wonder they were so poor. *Why did they have to be so goody goody?* Alpha's eyes had opened up to other alternatives when he joined the 'School for Rogues'. As his intention was to be in governance, he quickly embraced what the school meted out to him, in terms of their expectations, their aim and objectives and their hopes. *Now, now, Alpha, look where you've landed yourself.* But, being part of the system was he made to pay for his crimes? Nooo, not this rotten system, the rotten policy makers and rotten implementers did not allow Alpha to be prosecuted for rape, underage sex and any other thing for that matter but Alpha lived with the consequences of his actions as a full blown HIV/AIDS patient and to this day, lucid recollections of the full rounded breasts that he furiously assaulted, the tightness of her womanhood, the bruises that he received in his quest for primal satisfaction and the beautiful face of the 'not looking like fourteen year old' Sally were infinitely etched in his painfully anguished and perplexed mind.

A complex situation that presented itself to my brother, who like I had always rightfully considered too simple to understand life's rules that 'you get back what you give to the world'. How many more Sallys had been part of his immoral life? How many more Sallys had he infected with the dreaded virus? How many more Alphas are there who form part of the governance and public service arena and are alumni of the 'School for Rogues'? We therefore found ourselves in a situation of 'I told you so' both from our parents and myself. Why would you throw away a life of honesty and good morals? I then told him, "Alpha, I'll rather be seen as a fool, than be caught up in the trappings and the teachings of the 'School for Rogues'.

Alpha then wanted to settle down, marry and have children. That was the complex situation that he had on his hands.

Gbanabom Hallowell

A Place to Die

What better place to draw one's last breath than in the house of God? Sengbe Pieh, ecclesiastical of thought, had settled. With such a resolve, as was always known of him, the only other matter to overcome was to conquer the seven-forest-distant-long journey, between the village square he had just arrived at and the missionary compound, the locals had reminded him was up the gradient hill.

The villagers' consternation, brought about by Sengbe Pieh's haggard and ghostly look, had made them resort to manifesting their disapproval and rejection of his presence in their midst until he felt the pangs of their disgust, and went on his way from them.

At the age of eighty something years, the inevitable footpath of seven forests was more of an ache in his mind than it was on his already pinching and bare soles when he resumed his journey. The bouts of agony posed the cruelest challenge to his desire to reach the missionary compound. Taking one peripheral step after another was even more grueling than the distance he had to cover.

As he left the village, he realized with satisfaction that none of the locals knew who he really was. In the early months of his return from slavery in America, there was not a household in Sherbro and Mende lands that did not recognize him. He had grown tired of recalling those mundane moments, but only if his memory would help it. The sorrow of coming from the known hero to the unknown, even among his own people, from whom he was now fleeing, and seeking to find the church that had disowned him on his return to Africa, discomforted him like broken blades in his mouth.

In those early months of his return, just as everyone was clamouring to share the glory with him as the former Sherbro slave who had mutinied at sea, killed almost everyone of his captors, went to America and legally as well as 'magically' gained his freedom from the white man, Sengbe Pieh had suddenly disappeared. He had left to search for his wife and children, entrusting that information to no one.

When pain and continuous fresh desire to search for one's wife lurk forever in one's beleaguered mind, particularly at a ripe old age, it would always be difficult not to smell conspiracy in every other full blooded human being one crosses path with. For that matter, and the pains brought about by the absence of his family from Mende, Sengbe Pieh remained gloomy for the most part of his life on earth.

On his arrival at the village square, several forests of distance behind him, Sengbe Pieh had almost forgotten how much hunger had twisted his stomach when fatigue had forced him to slouch on the ground in the middle of the village square. Even before trying to know what creature he was, and where he was from, the villagers had crowdedly informed him that there was nowhere to put him up, even for the night, neither was there any leftover food for him, and that the best there was for him to do was to pick up himself and leave before the uglier citizens of the village returned from hunting and missed him for a lingering game that must be quickly shot at for supper.

Haggard as he was, Sengbe Pieh had accepted that only the church could afford to look after his person until called to lie down with his ancestors. But what other option was there for a man, his age, and having drained all the blood of hope and energy from his bones, to find comfort at such an old age and a peaceful deathbed?

If he was doomed not to ever see his beloved family of a wife and three children again, then let him die in the comfort of the church. He was angry at first that he should opt to seek refuge in a church that had once betrayed him. Was it not going to betray him again? After a while though, he had gone to a next level where the idea of seeking refuge in the church had been turned and turned over in his mind, perhaps by the power of a miraculous spirit, to a point where he agreed with his own spirit that only the church could bring about a dignified closure to his endless search for his family.

Sengbe Pieh was happy to realize that he eventually covered the seven forest distance that led to the church. Already, the familiar tower with the cross of Jesus at its apex was rising ahead of him. Even though he had not seen it for, at least, three decades, since he helped erect it on his return from slavery, he still remembered the mystery behind the gold crest image of the cross and the twinkling silver star resting on its tip. That afternoon, when the young American missionary climbed up the ladder to affix the Silver Star on the tip of the cross, Sengbe Pieh thought he saw a lengthy ray come from the brightness of the sun, and flashing across the Silver Star, and the hand of the missionary trembling like a reed. As he approached the missionary compound, the feeling of that same holiness returned to him as he stood in front of the colossal gate. For a moment, he stood still and wondered whether he was anymore that clean to seek clemency in the house of God. Suddenly, he felt an intense sense of hesitation and he backed away from the gate.

The only other time he had ever hesitated that much was in the schooner, the pirate ship that had stolen him from Komende. He remembered that after he and others had successfully unchained themselves at sea, and in the ensuing struggle between captors and captives, a young Spanish lad, under the instruction of a drunken adult Spanish man, had taken a knife to stab him in his face. He had grabbed the boy by his throat and shoved him off. The boy was told to advance with a bigger knife thrown to him by the much older Spaniard. Undecidedly, Sengbe Pieh had taken the boy down by his legs. He had hung the nail he had freed himself with over him. The boy could have been slightly older than his own son left in Africa. But with no sorrow, the boy had stabbed him from beneath him. He had groaned, and with all his might had dealt the boy a fatal blow. He knew he would never have killed the boy if it was not, for him, a matter of life and death.

Brought back from his thoughts, a heavy shower dropped on Sengbe Pieh, as if it was to further stop him from entering the missionary compound. The noise of the rain was so deafening that the loudest call and the hardest hit on the door did not bring anyone to respond to his knocking. Those who eventually heard it did not come to his aid. Instead, they scared him away from the door. A pack of dogs advanced at him so voraciously that he took to his heels seeking refuge in a nearby hut, which also provided him shelter from the uncompromising rain.

.

Pen, the young Black American Missionary in Komende, had just nearly finished having his supper when he thought he heard an unusual noise. He stepped away from his dining table, still chewing on a piece of mutton; he had an empty spoon in his hand. He was only three weeks in Komende, and was still regularly startled by any noise he heard. He walked to the front door and pressed his right ear to it. Indeed, there was coming from outside, the sound of banging on the gate.

It was dark outside and the wind was flailing. After a period of initial shock, Pen suspected that most of the noises were those of scavenging dogs barking, or some ritualistic pagan group performing a ceremony somewhere far away. However, the tormenting noise persisted and turned desperate.

The banging grew louder. In just three weeks after his arrival in Africa, Pen was already used to rescuing helpless locals from becoming fatal victims to some ritualistic lore. This might very well be one of those cases, he thought. He opened the door, and was swallowed by the harsh arrows of a black rain. Without picking a torch, he ran to the watchman's shed shouting at the top of his voice to wake him up from a sleep, dead and deep. The watchman was used to that kind of rude awakening from the young missionary ever since he was brought to the mission. So, without asking, he knew that any soul met at the gate was to be instantly rescued and dragged to the church of God. In an instant, he flung open the gate, and pulled into the compound the man who had been thumping on the gate. He guided the victim to the church and sat him in a pew.

Pen entered the church to be greeted by an old man.

"Who is our late night guest?" Pen questioned the watchman.

"I never knowed him, this man, and he nor look like anyone in the village. First time to see him meself, this man," the watchman said and began to excuse himself from Pen.

"Wait here, Joe," he told the watchman.

The watchman looked into the face of Pen before retreating to a corner to wait.

"Old man, do you speak English?" Pen hesitantly advanced toward Sengbe Pieh. When Sengbe Pieh did not answer, he turned to the watchman and asked, "Did you talk to him while bringing him to the church?"

"No, I not talk to him. I just help him walk to here," the watchman said.

"Could you ask him in Sherbro or Mende his name and what he wants with us?"

"That nor necessary, pastor. Me speak English too," Sengbe Pieh breathed.

Pen and the watchman edged themselves and stared at Sengbe Pieh.

"Me, I am Joseph Cinque. Africa here, me name Sengbe Pieh nor name Joseph Cinque," he said.

Pen still stood blank as if his biological clock had just been switched off.

"Me nor understand. You be Joseph Cinque, the long long Sherbro for American slave?" the watchman stepped in.

Pen shoved him aside, "That's okay, Joe. Let me handle this."

Sengbe Pieh stared at the watchman and said, "Yes, me, and me come here to die in peace."

Pen urged the watchman to go back to his post. He then sat on the adjacent pew. The watchman reluctantly walked outside the church door. Pen thought for a while, and assured the old man that he was in the house of God where people were treated with respect. He suggested to him that he first needed to eat something if he was feeling hungry. Sengbe Pieh hurriedly accepted. Pen asked Sengbe Pieh to accompany him to his apartment. He then remembered that he himself had not even finished his food when he had heard the thumping at the gate.

Back at his residence, after they had shared a meal, Pen took out a bottle of red wine and surprised Sengbe Pieh with a smile. By this time, Pen had begun warming up to Sengbe Pieh. Pen poured a huge glass for Sengbe Pieh and a moderate one for himself.

Sengbe Pieh had a bushy mouth with his moustache considerably hanging over his lips. He parted the top moustache with his forefingers and took a big sip of his wine. He withdrew the glass, looked into it deeply and took a second sip of it. He breathed out deeply as if he had also taken a puff from a pipe. He was a smoker, but didn't feel that he should ask to be given anything to smoke after the warm welcome he had already received.

"What a young American like you doing this part of me people's town alone?" Sengbe Pieh broke the silence.
"I am a missionary, a new missionary."

Pen wished he could instantly trust Sengbe Pieh the moment he disclosed he was Joseph Cinque, the man, whose astronomical and historical image had moved him to opt to serve in Africa after graduating as a young clergy from Morehouse College. Since meeting Sengbe Pieh, he had fought very hard to restrain his excitement. Was it indeed true that he was meeting Joseph Cinque?

He was a child when the *Amistad* arrived in New York and therefore did not get to see the drama that resulted to the freedom of Sengbe Pieh and others of his countrymen. Growing up in antebellum America of the servitude, for Pen and many others, the achievement of the enslaved people of the *Amistad*, was a heightened reality that the black man could fight for and gain his freedom from slavery.

Since then, Pen had grown up with a badge of hot iron inside his chest. He read voraciously and hungered after the guts and glory during his college days. Informed that as a free black man, the best opportunity for him to ever travel to Africa would be through the church, Pen decided to become a clergy.

"You wine, you not drinking you wine," Sengbe Pieh cut into Pen's thought.

Pen quickly fumbled with his glass, "Oh, I was just lost in thought..."

"About me, me know. Not you alone. Plenty people wonder too now, long time after me go search for me lost family."

"You lost your family?"

Sengbe Pieh instantly swallowed his throat.

"You lost your family in America or in Africa?"

"Lost family when went to slavery, see no family when me got back to Sherbro."

"Oh dear!"

"All me life me don look for family from Sherbro to Mende to Themne to the sea....but sea big, sea long."

An uneasy silence hung between them.

At once, Sengbe Pieh leaped from his seat, rushed to Pen and seized him by his cloak, "No, no, no, oh dear. Me nor give up on family, no, no, no. Me nor come here to die, me come to plead church to help me see me wife and children." He became hysterical, pulling off the cloak of Pen.

"You have to calm down old man, calm down!" Pen said croakily.

"The church keep me family from me all these years...please don't be like them...tell me where the church took me family."

Pen continued to struggle with Sengbe Pieh to free his cloak from his grip. Sengbe Pieh was wailing at the top of his voice. Suddenly, tthe rain resumed, more noisily than before. The door flew open as a heavy gust of wind entered the hall. Pen was finally able to free himself from Sengbe Pieh.

Sengbe Pieh became broken; he returned calmly to his seat as if to prepare for a final prayer. He searched for his glass, raised it to his face, but it was empty; nevertheless, he sipped from it and let it fall from his hand.

"You are drunk! I shouldn't have offered you more to drink. That's what it is...otherwise how can you accuse the church of stealing your family after all these years?" Pen shouted. "Have you come here for help or to accuse the church falsely about your missing family? In fact, how can anyone believe that you are indeed Joseph Cinque?" he continued.

Sengbe Pieh picked himself quietly from the pew and walked closer to Pen, "*Gboooow* young pastor, how long you been here. Me sweat be here in this church. We fix the cross up in the arch and we open this place to local people, me people, to come to prayer to God. After America make me free, me turn back home, here after the good man, good old man, Jo...John Kinsi Adams and all him friends fight hard for we. Some people stay back, we say we come back home. Me come back for me family, me wife and three children. The church say they help find me family. Five missionaries come with us for open *Mende Mission*. We open *Mende Mission* and nobody look for me family. Pastor, me come from very very far place and me search for me wife."

He slumped to the floor and cried. In that moment, he carefully unwrapped from the bottom of his gown, a wrinkled rectangular piece of hard paper, which he handed over to Pen.

Pen took the cold paper and returned to his chair under the lamp. The paper was wet. He quickly realized that he was holidng an engraving! He took a quick look at Sengbe Pieh who was still flung on the floor. The paper was dirty and he could see nothing more that it showed. He put it aside on the table and returned to Sengbe Pieh.

Already, Pen was moved by the words of Sengbe Pieh. He bent over him to pick him from the floor and return him to the chair. Instead, he looked into his eyes and said, "Who ever you are, you have arrived in the place where God wants you to bring a closure to your search for your family or for anything you ever lacked. Please let me find you a place to sleep. The church has been searching for you since you left the *Mende Mission*. You certainly have a long story to tell me."

Pen returned to his chair and for a while was lost in thoughts. The rain continued to pelt outside and a violent storm could be heard banging on doors and windows. As he leaned, his left hand nearly knocked down the lamp and the paper Sengbe Pieh had given him. He decided to take a keener look at it again. He saw an unclear engraving on the paper. He began to make out the image of a man holding a staff. Below the image, he saw written, *The Chief of the Amistad Captives*. He trembled, grabbed his glasses from his study and brought out a bigger lamp. He studied the paper more closely and thought he saw a young man leaping from it! Startled, he ran backwards and stumbled on Sengbe Pieh. Sengbe Pieh sprawled motionless across the floor!

Harriet Yeanoh Jones

Kadiatu

The Arrival

When Mum came back home, that evening, she was greeted by the sight of a little girl coiled up in one of the armchairs in the sitting room. She was fast asleep, and she looked somehow knackered.

"She is indeed tired," remarked her uncle who had been waiting patiently to formally present the young stranger to Mum. "She'd never stepped out of her village before and besides, this is the longest journey she has ever made," he continued.

"What's her name?" Mum asked.

"Kadiatu," he replied. "Kadiatu Isatu Kamara," he pronounced each of the names carefully.

As Mum continued asking about other personal details, she carefully perused the little girl's face. It looked unattractive to her—a dark skinned girl, about the age of ten or younger, with short black hair. After having taken in some details, it was as if Mum said to herself, "I am going to have her all to myself. There's plenty of time for me to study her physical features, as well as every other bit of her makeup."

"How old is she?" Mum asked, eyes still feasting on the girl's visible features.

"I am not certain," the uncle replied, "However, I shall try to get that detail from her father as soon as possible." He wiped the sweat that had begun to form on his forehead with the back of his left hand. Mum went on to ask whether Kadiatu had a birth certificate. It was at that point that she learnt that Kadiatu's father was educated, and, therefore, could not afford to treat such matters with levity. Ali, for that was the uncle's name, promised faithfully that he would go back to the village as soon as he could to collect the birth certificate from Kadiatu's father. Mum was not surprised to learn that Kadiatu was already enrolled in school, and that she was in class three, given the fact that the father was not only an educated man, but one who was occupied with the business of imparting knowledge to children in the community.

Uncle Ali left shortly after Kadiatu had gone to bed, and he himself was satisfied that he had answered the questions that required immediate responses. That first night, Kadiatu slept like a log. By 6 o'clock the next morning, she was up. Mum showed her the bathroom as she definitely needed to sort herself out. Mum watched with keen interest as the little girl painstakingly washed various parts of her body in preparation for prayers. This was something she had obviously learnt from her parents.

"Kadiatu, you needn't do all of that anymore. You are now in a different environment," Mum said. After she left the bathroom, Kadiatu wanted to say good morning to Mum and Dad. How could she? She could only speak *Themne* which no one else in the household understood; every other person in the household spoke *Krio*, a language that was completely strange to her. That barrier remained a problem for weeks. It was a constraint on the one hand for the family and a source of frustration on the other for Kadiatu. She could neither interact verbally with the rest of the family nor could they interact with her. The other little girls, her age, also found it somewhat difficult to interact with her. Whenever they spoke to her, she just stared vaguely at them. Apart from the frustration Kadiatu was battling with, she was also missing her parents, siblings, playmates, and other people with whom she was used to speaking. *Now it was all so strange*, Kadiatu thought. Indeed, back in the village, there was a lot of work, however, her life and that of the other villagers were finely spiced up with some kind of incomprehensible bliss: going to the stream with the elders and other children to fish or fetch water; going to the farm in the early hours of the morning to weed or scare birds; not having much to do in harvest festivities or in the preparation of the late evening meals—it was better for Kadiatu than this cage of luxury in which she now found herself. The effect it had on her was quite tremendous.

As the days went by and things continued to unfold, Mum became a bit baffled. She found it hard to figure out how a child who had absolutely no knowledge of English could be in class three. As a matter of fact, the prescribed texts were all written in English. She had many doubts about this young girl for which she needed clarification. What shocked Mum even the more was when Ali explained that there were certain schools in the remote parts of Sierra Leone that were not following the prescribed government calendar. "Community life or nature dictates," he had said. He equally had said, whenever there was a bountiful harvest, school could be closed temporarily as both teachers and pupils had to be involved in farm activities. For these people, school was not much perceived as a means of empowerment. "After all, these people have led happy lives without schools," Ali had ended jokingly.

Such was the life led by Kadiatu in the village. As Mum got to understand these peculiarities, her state of bafflement gradually disappeared.

A New Family

In the Moyamba district, Southern province of Sierra Leone, there was a small village called Mochail, Kadiatu's birth place. There she had lived in a small hut with her parents, five siblings, uncles, aunts, and grandparents. Sheep and chickens with which they had shared the hut were not counted. But they were happy. This union, Kadiatu missed very much.

"Kadiatu, you are going to Freetown, a very big city where a better life awaits you," her father had told her.

"Your uncle has met someone loving who has promised to take good care of you," he had ended with a broad grin.

Kadiatu was saddened by the news. She did not want to leave her parents, siblings and friends but her father's dictates were to be followed no matter what. Besides, her father had told her Uncle Ali himself lived in Freetown and would be checking on her from time to time; she had felt a bit assured of security. Isatu Kamara, Kadiatu's mother, was not very pleased to see her young daughter go to such a big and dangerous city but the promise of a better life and the hope of a secured future had made her to let the child go, even though reluctantly. They had gone to consult the "medicine man". In that community, religious and traditional leaders were highly revered; therefore, whatever utterances they made were always treated with utmost seriousness. When the 'medicine man' predicted of a brighter future, Kadiatu's mother no longer harboured any hesitation to let her daughter go to the big city.

Kadiatu and her uncle had, therefore, left the seaside village of Mochail on a Sunday afternoon for the capital city of Sierra Leone. They travelled by boat and arrived at Fogbo. At Fogbo, they boarded a vehicle for Waterloo, where they boarded another vehicle which took them into the heart of the city of Freetown. Indeed, it was all strange for Kadiatu. She now found herself trapped in a maze of big and beautiful buildings compared to the tiny huts in her village. Her new home had few people, and they were Christians. She, coming from a community which was strongly rooted Islam, found it difficult to follow the Christian life. In her new environment, education was viewed as a key to life's success. Nearly every other aspect was done differently in both communities.

At first, it appeared as if Kadiatu would never cope. She cried for days on end. One day, Mum almost sent her back to the village, but she called Uncle Ali and told him about Kadiatu's difficulty in settling down. On one occasion, Kadiatu took the black plastic bag she had brought along with her from the village and attempted to run away but was caught by a neighbour, Michael, who told her that she would be eaten up by cannibals if she did not return home. It was that threat that made her run back home. Mum found the situation a bit disheartening; she had done all she could to get Kadiatu integrated, all to no avail. Kadiatu still wanted to go back to the village. She stayed isolated from the other children, singing *Temne* songs from time to time. No matter what Mum did, she could clearly recall one common expression: *Mine I yemakone do mama*, meaning she wanted to go to her mother. What Mum found interesting in all of this was that Kadiatu would consume every bit of food she was given, and then continued with her crying, interspersed with singing. She never, for once, rejected anything she was offered to eat or drink. When Kadiatu heard the message from her father that she never was going back to the village, she realized, with frustration, that she was in the city for good and gradually had to change her attitude. She began to note the beautiful things which were absent in her village.

Adaptation

As days, weeks and months went by; Kadiatu began to feel at ease in her new environment. She began to have much fun and laughter. There were happy moments, interesting moments, and even sour moments. As she acquired the lingua franca, she became livelier in her interactions with everyone. A great impediment to her social life had gradually disappeared—the language barrier. She could confidently communicate with everyone around, apparently finding joy and happiness in this her new family. But certain dishes still posed difficulties for Kadiatu, for she was not used to eating salad which for her was merely a combination of 'uncooked leaves'. However, with time, she grew to like them even better than the African dishes she had been used to. Mum could vividly recall when she once said to her, "Mama, we are going to prepare *Jollof* rice, don't forget to buy the vegetables to garnish it." Mum could not help but laugh. Mum said to her, "You seem to like vegetables more than everyone else."

"Yes, I really like vegetables especially cabbage and carrot," she answered with a broad grin. Sunday after Sunday, Kadiatu would be so excited to dress up in her fineries to go to church. She was completely adapted. Once, when she was in a light-hearted mood, she had said to Mum, "I enjoy singing hymns. I find them soul refreshing. That is one of the reasons why I like orthodox churches." Initially, Mum had thought she had gone too far but when she sought the consent of Kadiatu's parents on the issue of going to church, she was relieved to know that they were not worried about the change. As far as they were concerned, Kadiatu's general wellbeing superseded all other matters, even extending to that of religion.

In all this, there were happy and interesting moments and there were sour or not so pleasant moments. Kadiatu had started school, a stone's throw away from her new home. She was admitted into class two. Mum had suggested that Kadiatu be placed in class two because she had a rather weak foundation. Even in class three, the class she was in, in her village school, she could neither write properly all the letters of the alphabet nor could she sound them. Writing figures one to twenty was a task that equally posed difficulty. That was why Mum was really taken aback and she became angry when she learnt from one of her nieces in the same school as Kadiatu that she stoutly refused to stand with the other class two children during morning devotion but would rather join the class three children. Kadiatu would tell them that she belonged to class three and therefore would never stand with them. It was after some warning and counselling from Mum that she had agreed to stand with the class two children during devotion. In Kadiatu's new family, study time was a daily activity. Every child had to study for at least an hour or two. This was an experience that Kadiatu had found most undesirable. She would grumble, frown and even shed tears whenever it was study time. Once, she was even bold enough to say that she wasn't going to do the exercises assigned to her. She was not used to this kind of rigorous training. For her, study time merely meant looking at pictures and flipping through the pages of books. But things were not going to change so she eventually succumbed to them.

On certain evenings, when Kadiatu was in high spirits, she would narrate some interesting incidents or general happenings in her village. The amazing part of it was that she would even condemn certain things she had been enjoying or of which she had been a part in the village. The ideal was what she now saw in her environment. For instance, here cassava leaves were not pounded but done by a machine. Tasks were carried out here less laboriously. To her, things were much more impressive in the city. There were big shops and supermarkets all over the place. In school, Kadiatu was an average pupil; a persevering learner who was loved by all her teachers. She had grown to be civil and neat. Whenever children of her age and perhaps some a bit older came around, she would raise the bed covering which usually draped over the bed to display her collection of footwear.

That was her subtle way of showing off. At the uppermost level of her primary school career, she became one of the fond girls of her teachers. Of course, this was something she never told Mum about. With the regular supervision she received at home and the teaching in school, Kadiatu did fairly well at the National Primary School Examination (NPSE), and she was admitted into the Freetown Secondary School for Girls (FSSG). There again, because of her pleasant disposition, she was loved by her teachers and friends. Kadiatu continued working hard; when she took the Basic Education Certificate Examination (BECE) she was admitted into the senior section of FSSG.

Kadiatu had grown into a beautiful young lady; tall and dark with black hair and bulging eyes, and she still loved to dress well. In the evenings, she would take her second bath and dress up in clean clothes. After finishing her chores for the day, she would pick up her books to study, and she would go on until she finally fell asleep. She also found time to relax; watching movies. From time to time, she would sit with her peers and together they would discuss topics of interest.

Five years after Kadiatu joined her new family, a new member was added, a baby brother. Kadiatu's love for her baby brother was so great. In fact, both of them were fond of each other. They would hug and play with each other. One could actually see that they enjoyed each other's company in spite of the age difference; just one of the reasons Mum thought of Kadiatu as the perfect girl. She (Mum) was sometimes considered impatient and very intolerant but Kadiatu was always full of praises for her. In any case, Harry and Kadiatu's relationship could be compared to that of "Mary and the Little Lamb." Kadiatu also had a sister with whom she shared company; the one who had been around before Harry was born. Ethel was that sister. Naturally, Ethel and Kadiatu would quarrel every now and then over nothing. Sometimes, they refused to speak to each other but Mum would always intervene and keep things in check. In spite of all that, the relationship between Kadiatu and Harry grew. When school choice forced Harry to relocate to the provinces, Kadiatu could not resist shedding tears. But things soon became normal. She was happy in her new family, and she coped splendidly. The hub of the family, she was fun to be with; full of humour, telling little jokes that made everyone wriggle with laughter.

A Sad Day
One evening, Uncle Ali came on one of his regular visits. Apparently, he had just come back from the village. He brought with him two fat cocks and a gallon of palm oil. These were gifts sent by Kadiatu's mother as a token of her appreciation. Uncle Ali told Mum that both parents had sent their warmest regards, and that they were very pleased with the feedback they were receiving about Kadiatu's wellbeing. Of course, Uncle Ali had always been giving them regular update. After all the pleasantries, Uncle Ali sat for a while before finally dropping the bombshell!

"Kadiatu's parents sent me to seek permission on their behalf so that together with her peers she could be initiated into the *Bondo* society."

"It's really not a bad idea," Mum had replied thoughtfully.

"The only problem here is that I would have loved them to wait until she takes the WASSCE."

Mum then emphasized she was not imposing her own idea but merely making a suggestion. That was the message Mum asked Uncle Ali to take back to Kadiatu's parents. In a very calm manner, Uncle Ali had responded that he'd do just as Mum had requested. Kadiatu was not present when that discussion between Mum and Uncle Ali took place. After

Uncle Ali had gone, Mum called her and informed her about her parents' wish. Before Mum finished the explanation, Kadiatu burst into tears. Not that she had a problem with the initiation ceremony; in fact, she hadn't the faintest idea of what it really involved. As far as she was concerned, it was merely fun and enjoyment. It was a time for dressing up in fineries and receiving special treatment. All of that was quite all right. What had saddened her was the fact that she was going back to the village. In her little mind, she had thought perhaps she would not be coming back to the city. She had feared she might be given in marriage to an old man in the village, and that she would eventually drop out of school. Mum was really surprised. She sat speechless looking at Kadiatu as she sobbed. After a few minutes, Mum told her to calm down and listen. Mum then told her what she had told Uncle Ali.

"As it stands, we are waiting for their response to my suggestion, and I am convinced we'll get a positive one," Mum had assured her.

"Stop doing this to yourself," Mum had continued. After some intermittent outbursts she finally kept quiet. Even though she had stopped crying, she was in a sombre mood for the rest of the day. She could not laugh; she could not play like she used to, and on that particular day she retired early to her bed. She might have even dreamt about everything that happened on that day especially when her fate was yet undecided.

A Ray of Hope
Two weeks on, Uncle Ali came back from the village. His presence created anxiety in Kadiatu. What could her parents have said in response? Would she really be going to the village? Did her parents give Mum's suggestion a serious

56

thought? But they had given her to this family and she had agreed to be a member. Whatever the case, her new family's say should be final. Such were the thoughts pricking her mind. She could neither sit down nor stay in one place. She kept pacing up and down under the pretext of doing some work, but she meant to eavesdrop. Her heart throbbed so hard. Uncle Ali sat in a rather relaxed manner, his face lightened up with a smile. He talked about quite a few things but none had to do with Kadiatu. Mum didn't want to jump the gun, so she waited patiently as the conversation continued. Finally Uncle Ali came out with it.

"The young lady's parents think your suggestion is a good one and have therefore consented to defer Kadiatu's initiation to a later date."

Mum jumped and immediately called Kadiatu to share the glad tidings with her. Kadiatu's face lit up with joy. She was more than pleased with what she heard. Once again, she became buoyant. She knew she'd definitely have to go to the village in due course, if not for anything, but to bond with her parents and siblings. Mum equally wanted Kadiatu to understand she had an identity, and, therefore, must not run away from her roots. That was something very serious for Mum; the reason she had always consulted Kadiatu's parents on sensitive issues.

Kadiatu's determination multiplied; determined to succeed in life, looking into the future with hope.

Kadiatu will soon face the WASSCE. She hopes to become a nurse. With fingers crossed, the family views the beam in sight ...

James Bernard Taylor

Falling Leaves

"I'll kill you," Fatu screamed as she rolled over and sat on Adeline's chest, hitting her repeatedly on the head with her shoe. Adeline struggled to cough up a reply but found herself gasping. She forced out a helpless, *'Lef...'* choked back with sobs and her heavier breathing. Gathering all the strength she could muster, she heaved and managed to flip Fatu over. The wrestling women rolled along the veranda as they struggled and hit themselves against the rails. Blood streamed down Adeline's face as Fatu continued to hit her. The blows came repeatedly and Fatu was full of strength that day so Adeline found it difficult to match her force. After struggling to no avail, Adeline sank her teeth into Fatu's left thigh. Fatu screamed as the pain surged through her, weakening her hold and halting her bludgeoning of Adeline's head.

A crowd of spectators had formed a ring outside the house as the drama went on. Unconsciously, they had divided themselves into two groups of supporters—each one applauding their side whenever their wrestler took the advantage. When Adeline sank her teeth into Fatu's leg, a group of rowdy women shouted in excitement, "Pull! Pull! Pull them out, Adeline." It was clear that Adeline's five-foot, hundred-pound frame couldn't match Fatu's hefty figure but the crowd refused to interfere. Fatu continued to crush and blanket Adeline on the ground. At Grassfield Town, it was usual for people not to intervene in fights, even when danger was imminent. This was because those involved in any form of quarrel would hurl expletives against those who might want to intervene. So the crowd watched from a safe distance, faces lit up with excitement as the two women tore each other apart. Satisfied she had battered her opponent into submission Fatu dealt her final blow, got up and walked triumphantly into the house.

Adeline lay still as blood oozed from her wounds. The crowd watched fearfully hoping Adeline would get up but she lay still. Fearing the worst, everyone hurriedly dispersed. Soon after, Brer Mello came out of the house, picked Adeline up and carried her in like a crumpled bundle. With the help of some people who had found the courage to intervene, she was given CPR and ice cubes were placed on her forehead, which eventually revived her. Fatu, fearing that she had killed Adeline, had sneaked out through the back door and found a place to hide. Brer Mello was terribly angry. Were it not for a friend who had sent to call him; his house would have made the news again. Hurriedly, he had dispersed some of his men to search for Fatu. Meanwhile, the thinning crowd had swelled again and everybody was chattering about the incident. At this time of the day, Congo Market was a busy place. The residents of this tiny section of Grassfield, in the west of Freetown, were always busy on Saturday evenings. The activities would usually start the previous evening. This was the time when all the local bars would be in full operation and the people from surrounding neighbourhoods normally would have a good time. Congo Market doubled as a commercial and social centre, and weekends were very wild. To take part in all the activities, some people would sell their belongings, even their household items, on the cheap. They would spend the money drinking and dancing through the night. Brer Mello had a small bar in his two-storeyed house, which he had built from the fortune he made at sea. Not having finished primary school, he had come up the hard way, doing menial jobs before landing a fishing boat deckhand job that he had made good use of. He had always brought home cartons of fish for his mother to sell. Brer Mello had been displaced when rebels attacked his village in the Eastern province and both his parents were killed. Having no idea where his other relatives were, he had come to Freetown, where he roamed the city looking for odd jobs. Homeless, hungry and alone he turned into a pickpocket. Those were difficult times, Brer Mello thought. Now, he was one of the few provincial people who mattered in Congo Market, and he was the envy of his peers. Girls and women flocked around him; the educated, the illiterate, employed, and unemployed, *aristos* and the low class. None of them minded, as long as Brer Mello was willing to part with some of his cash, and which they all needed as things were difficult at Grassfield Town. As a small boy in Freetown, Mello had hustled his way to success. One particular day, things had gone sour. That was over fifteen years ago. On that particular day, his best plan of taking something home to his roommates had failed him. He had sat on a wooden stool at King Jimmy market, his mind straying to imaginary kingdoms and palaces. He removed the matchstick from his left ear, rubbed it on his torn T-shirt and hissed. He had not cleaned his ears for months now. There was no time for such a thing; finding food and shelter was more pressing. He stood at the corner of the market, scratching his itchy ears and unconsciously twisting a loose end of his ragged T-shirt with his right hand. The sixteen-square-foot room he shared with three other friends was like a graveyard, with each confined to his own rectangular space. The windowless room boasted a single, cardboard door. All they had were a few torn mats and four nails screwed on the back of the door, where their clothes were hung. They had allowed him to stay after he pleaded with them for a whole week. He had constantly wondered when his lot would improve.

61

As always, he directed his fifteen-year-old mind to the day ahead of him. He watched as people moved along the busy streets and into King Jimmy Market. It was 10 am and the sun was already high in the sky. His slim, 5 feet 7-inch frame had made it easy for him to navigate through thick crowds like a snake on grass. He could easily steal from the pockets and purses of passers-by. But that Saturday morning had seemed unpromising. It was in the middle of January and it was easy to connect the despondent look on the people's faces to the bare state of their pockets and purses. Most people were still reeling from the effects of Christmas spending. But he had to make a living; he had to take something to his roommates.

Suddenly, his attention was drawn to a middle-aged woman holding a basket. She was plump, wearing a loose cotton top and brown *lappa*. He waited for the lady to go past him, and then he followed discreetly, observing her every move. He was sure this was the opportunity he was looking for.

"Yes!" he said to himself. He moved closer to his prey, walked by her side and peeped into her basket. Mello was disappointed when he saw nothing but old towels. Crestfallen, he had turned away. Then, all of a sudden, realizing that most of these women keep their money in their bosoms, Mello developed a renewed interest and lifted his head towards the lady's chest. The impressions of a loaded purse were clearly visible, so he kept his pace and moved closer, as his heart hit against his ribs like a pestle on a mortar. With nobody paying attention to him, he had quickly put his hand on the woman's blouse. But his hand, seized by the woman, came out clutching her left breast. All eyes turned to him as the woman screamed,

"Put it in again! Nobody asked you to take it out! You thieves have turned the city upside down, but today, you have met your Waterloo."

Mello remembered shaking with embarrassment. He was so ashamed that his fear had paled into the background. He knew that, at worse, he would get a beating from the crowd, probably be arrested by the police and released later. It was routine; caught, beaten and/or arrested and released. But this time, he was caught holding a woman's breast in full view of everybody. How could he put it back in her blouse? The woman did not seem to mind. She was more desperate to teach him a lesson than worry about her exposed breast. But a solid slap from the woman had made him hastily drop her pound of flesh. Meanwhile, a small crowd had gathered, itching to lay hands on him but he was lucky. A passing policeman had hastily hauled him away from the mob. The policeman was looking for a much greener pasture. Mello's case was not a profitable one. Why take a miserable man to the station? After searching the young man thoroughly with the hope of draining him of whatever little he might have stolen, the policeman had released him with a sigh. All he had found was a shrivelled up piece of bread.

All this happened almost fifteen years ago. Mello's life was different now. I survived, Mello thought.

"What the hell is going on here? Congo Market is never tired," shouted someone in the crowd.

"It is not your business. You don't know what had happened?" another replied.

That started an exchange that brought Mello back from his reverie. His house now attracted many people, most of whom were traders and a few customers of his. The arguments continued for a while then an old man made a speech that temporarily tempered down the arguments.

"Ladies and Gentlemen, you don't know these ladies and what had happened to them. They are not strangers to each other. If you promise to be patient and quiet, I'll tell you all I know about them."

Pa Cole, for that was the old man's name, seemed to know everything in Grassfield. His eighty-year-old brain had never got tired of recording and storing information. His delivery of oral tales was something nobody ever wanted to miss. He was the custodian of the community's secrets. One after the other, people surrounded Pa Cole who had taken a posture on a mound of that dusty road to tell them another story. This time it was about Fatu.

"Fatu was brought into the household of the Johnsons when she was only seven years old. That was about twenty years ago. Fatu's mother, Ya Alimamy, had left Morlai Conteh, Fatu's father, and never returned. Morlai found it difficult to raise Fatu and had appealed to Mrs. Grace Johnson to take the child and raise her. Mrs. Johnson had sought the approval of her husband, Omotayo and they had agreed to take Fatu in. This was because Morlai had been a trusted manservant in the house of Mr. and Mrs. Johnson, where he had worked for about ten years. Morlai was not able to raise little Fatu now that he was not keeping well. He was dying of lung cancer and he lacked the money to even buy his drugs, let alone bring Fatu up. Fatu was happy to stay with the Johnsons. It was not a strange place to her, as she had often accompanied her father to work. She readily found a friend and playmate in the four-year-old Adeline, the daughter of the Johnsons and was very happy to make Adeline her sister and confidant. Mrs. Johnson, being a teacher, spent time with the children every evening, reading stories to them and teaching them to read."

"This shows that Mrs Johnson was a very nice woman," somebody interjected.

"It was because she wanted Fatu to do all the housework," another put in.

People started taking sides and the murmuring grew.

"If you continue to interrupt me, I'll leave," the old man threatened.

"Please don't leave," an enthusiastic lady pleaded.

"Well," Pa Cole continued, "Fatu loved Adeline and they grew up as sisters, going to school together and wearing similar dresses and shoes. Mr. Johnson never hesitated to buy things Fatu wanted. Morlai equally would bring things for Fatu whenever he afforded it, which was often rare. Not that he needed to; he just wanted to feel part of the team bringing his daughter up.

As time went on, things happened that changed the lives of the children for good."

The crowd edged closer, nobody wanting to miss this part of the story. Pa Cole drew a market table close and leaned against it, as the crowd waited with bated breath for him to continue.

"One late afternoon, after school, whilst the two children were eating, Adeline did something that was to change the relationship between the two children forever. She spat in the food. They were eating from the same plate, but Fatu was paying attention to one of the ants struggling to get a grain into its hole. Adeline didn't expect Fatu to notice, but as she spat in the food, Fatu raised her head and saw her. She ran to Mum, as Mrs. Johnson was fondly called, to report the incident. Adeline followed close by. After Fatu had told Mum of the incident, Adeline, being a crafty girl, immediately told a lie that Fatu was the one who spat in the food. Mum believed Adeline and gave Fatu a good beating. From then on, Mrs.

Johnson called Fatu a witch, accusing the girl of attempting to kill her daughter. Things got worse for Fatu. She now did the more difficult chores in the house whilst Adeline was given the less difficult ones. She failed twice in school, allowing Adeline to catch up with her."

At this point, there was suppressed but audible mumbling. Pa Cole looked around the crowd in a way that warned he would stop if the mumbling continued.

"Five years later, the girls graduated from high school. Each of them succeeded in securing a pass, although their grades were not good enough to enter college. But the friendship had already been severed. Fatu didn't want to stay in the house anymore and was searching for the slightest opportunity to move out. It was at this point that she met Mello. Mello provided her with comfort and care so she ran away from home and stayed with him. After two days, Mello asked Fatu to stay with his elder sister at the other end of Grassfield Town, far from the Johnson residence. Not too long after Fatu left, things became difficult for the Johnson family. Mr. Johnson lost his job at the Town Management Council where he had been working as an accountant. Two years later, he died of stress and Adeline was left with her mother who found it very difficult to fend for the family as a teacher. Adeline grew into a woman, light-skinned and beautiful. Mello got attracted to her, knowing that he already had Fatu."

"Ayyyyyy," a small boy giggled. He was topless. Pa Cole turned toward him and scolded,

"That's all that you are interested in these days, you young boys. You don't see your equals here, do you? Disappear before I get hold of you."

The boy became silent and his grin disappeared. A man standing close to him shoved his head and he left where he was standing, embarrassed.

"Anyway," Pa Cole continued, "Brer Mello was unaware that Fatu and Adeline had grown up together, and neither of the ladies knew Brer Mello was seeing the other. Mrs. Johnson became ill and died and Adeline was left to her fate. She became more and more dependent on Brer Mello."

It was getting late and the Harmattan breeze had started to blow, shedding leaves from the nearby trees. The old man was getting tired, but the crowd was even the more excited.

"What was Fatu doing as a means of livelihood?" an elderly woman asked arms akimbo.

Pa Cole turned to her, pursed his lips and shook his head. "Fatu was a hairdresser and she had a private business at home where she was staying with Brer Mello's sister."

"How come both of them met today?" a seemingly drunken, middle-aged man inquired rather brashly, but Pa Cole paid him no heed. He just continued with his story.

"Fatu came to see Brer Mello for some money," a voice interrupted. Everybody turned the direction of the voice to see it was that of the bare-skinned boy Pa Cole had driven away earlier on. The old man, by the boy's interruption, was relieved to have the question answered. The boy did not stop, he continued.

"She met Adeline talking to Brer Mello. A heated argument ensued and the old rivalry between the two ladies led to what we just saw."

By this time, the wind had grown stronger, swaying the branches of the trees. Suddenly, there was a loud cry. It was Fatu, held on either side by two of Brer Mello's men, with a small crowd following. They moved towards Brer Mello's house. The crowd's attention shifted to Fatu and her captors, eager to see what would happen next.

Just before the crowd broke up, a middle-aged woman asked jokingly,

"Pa Cole how did you know all that?"

Pa Cole smiled then answered, "I am the uncle of Mr. Omotayo Johnson, the father of Adeline, and I was with my nephew until he died." Pa Cole shook his head sadly and walked slowly toward Brer Mello's house, the crowd following behind.

Lef = *stop; omolay* = local brew; *aristos* = inherently rich people; *lappa* = loose cloth worn by women around the waste.

Jedidah Adlyn Olayinka Johnson

Letter to My Beloved

"No date but let the Love I have represent the date, for this, my love knows no time, knows no place and has no end."

Do you remember this is how I addressed the letters I used to write to you. The letters I wrote long ago when I was a child and in my childish eyes, you were an angel. An angel God sent for me. I would wake up very early in the morning and, before starting my chores, would scribble my thoughts on a little paper in the faint light of our kerosene lamp. I would tell you, once again, how beautiful you were. I would tell you how special you were and how much you meant to me. I would pour my thoughts out to you until I felt my mother's prying stare besides me on the mat we shared. I would hurriedly conclude then. Always with the same words! This is just one of those letters I used to write to you, my beloved. Then, I would carefully tuck the letter in the pages of one of my school books and wait for my mum's voice to say "Get up Momoh! You need to get ready for school".

I always smile to myself when I think of those happy moments. I would let my guard down for a moment and memories of you would inevitably come rushing back to enslave my senses and bring me the pain I had spent years trying to shield myself from. Years I had spent devoting myself to work and convincing myself that I hated you, that you had betrayed me and that I would someday find someone who would mean as much to me as you did. For fifteen years, I had convinced myself of this, carefully building walls to shield myself from your memories, and in a day, I had felt my carefully built fortress giving way. Like some addict, rehabilitated, I had felt myself thrust into a party surrounded by alcohol and booze, and I now realize I was not strong enough to resist. Back in Kenema, where I first met you; where our childish feelings first grew into a love that was true, I had almost felt like screaming "I still love you, Egertina George!"

What good would screaming do? These words that are still priceless were carried away by the wind and faded into nothingness. The same nothingness I have felt each night for the past fifteen years. I would sigh and suddenly feel like Paul, the fish scales dropping from my eyes. Ignoring these feelings would never erase them. I know what I must do. I must write a letter like the ones I used to write you. Not as a boy, now as a man; a man who has loved you every day for most of his life. Another letter to add to countless ones I had already written. Just another letter to you, my beloved, my beautiful Egertina George. So I lie down not on a mat this time but on a comfortable bed, not in our run down house made of corrugated iron sheets but in this expensive five star hotel. I take a pen and start to write.

No date but let the Love I have represent the date, for this, my love knows no time, knows no place, and has no end.

Egertina, I am writing you this letter though I do not know where you are and I am almost certain you will never read it. I am back in Kenema, and everything reminds me of your flawless beauty, your perfect smile and how happy you once made me. Today, feeling bored with being caged up in my hotel room, watching the lives of the *Kardashians*, I had taken a walk. I walked along the familiar roads and marveled at what changes had taken place. Dusty roads were now tarred and expanded. Where little houses with mud bricks and thatched roofs had once stood, were now brick-buildings; several stories high. Everything seemed so different and yet so familiar. I had walked the length and breadth of this town even before I met you, my feet had moved as though they were independent of the rest of my body. They had led me to a small corner on Blama Road. To my amazement, I had realized that this corner had hardly changed. I saw the same dilapidated houses made of corrugated iron sheets closely packed together in a compound where children's voices filled the air, where little boys played as I had once done in this same compound. I was transfixed as I watched and then, all of a sudden, a woman's voice rang out, "Abu, Abu come and help me". As the scene shone before my eyes, I was carried back in time. I saw myself the little boy again and I heard my mother's voice "Momoh, Momoh, come and help me." I had immediately dropped the ball I had been kicking around and run to her. "Yes mother, what do you want?" My mother had looked up from where she was cooking and pleaded, "Momoh, please carry a bag of coal to Aunty Kadie. She had already paid and I promised to send the coal this evening". The bag of coal was heavy but I did not complain. I had just put the bag on my head and started the walk. It was just another hot day in March and I had no clue I was to have a life-altering experience. I had passed along a familiar road by a familiar house. The house was well known by almost everybody in Kenema. It was a huge, beautiful house that had remained empty for several years since no one could afford to pay the rent. As a child, I had wondered what it would be like to live in a place so luxurious. As I passed by the house, I had noticed that the gates were open and a beautiful red car was parked in front of the gate. My curiosity made me forget the heavy load on my head and I stood to watch. I had seen your father come out of the vehicle. He was an impressive looking man. He had worn what I now would recognize as a fancy designer suit. Then, your mother had stepped out; she was beautiful and I looked on in awe. They had turned and seen a dirty boy with a bag of coal on his head staring at them. They did turn up their noses at me but I did not care. I still had looked on in awe. Then finally you had walked out, a vision in a pink dress with golden flowers. Your hair was set in beautiful curls and your face was flawless. I remember thinking you were an angel. You just had to be, for ordinary people did not look that way or smile the way you did when you saw me. Then, in that small voice that has haunted me every night for the past fifteen years, you had said, "Mother, look at that dirty boy" and then you had smiled again in enthrallment. I knew you meant no harm but I was suddenly ashamed of the way I looked. Your mother said then, in a harsh voice that sent me scurrying away, "Go away little thief". I should have known then that nothing good could come out of knowing you that I would never be the man you deserved; the man your parents would accept, but I was blinded by your beauty, your humanity. I should have forgotten all about you then, but I couldn't. It did not matter then if I spent the hour or so it took me to get back home or the past fifteen years I have spent trying to become the success I am today; trying to forget you. I have never been able to.

As soon as I got home, I had gone to Mama and said, "Mama I saw an angel today". She had laughed at my innocence but I had continued earnestly, "It is true, Mama; she is coming to live in that big house at Hanga Road". Mother smiled then and said, "She must be Dr. George's daughter. Her father is going to head the Government Hospital here. In fact, they need a maid and I would start working there tomorrow". I was ecstatic. "Then I would be able to see her, Mama, and we can be friends," I had said happily. Mama had looked into my eyes, held my shoulders with both of her hands, smiled again and softly muttered, "I don't think so… like you said, she is an angel and you are not". In those words were a thousand warnings. I should never have fallen in love with you or rather I should never have met you because the moment I met you the rest was inevitable.

We then became friends and then we realized that our parents did not want us to be friends so we became secret friends. We had seen each other whenever we could but mostly we had written letters. You had told me about your life. You had told me about your fancy toys and how bored you were with them. You had told me you just wanted to go out and play but you were not allowed to. I had in turn told you about the birds and the flowers and how they grew in the forest. I had told you how beautiful you were and you in turn had told me you didn't feel that way. You had let me into your world and had told me your insecurities. I had told you about my little house, my dear mother and my public school. You had mentioned your private school and had lamented that you could not make friends since everyone was so snobbish. I then promised you that you would forever find a friend in me. I had told you I loved you and you had said the same to me. You were the daughter of a doctor; I was a son of his maid. You were *Krio* and I was *Temne*. We were light years apart but you ended your letters with these words "I am forever yours. I am your Egertina". Some nights, I would sneak out, while my mother was asleep, and run all the way to your house. I would climb the fence and find my way to your room window. I would then whistle and you would open the window. I would be standing in front of you and in those instances, I knew perfect bliss. Egertina, as we grew older and bolder, we had met in the woods. Few stolen hours shared by two people in love. I remember the exact spot I had first kissed you. I remember where I had stood when I swore to love you a day after eternity. Egertina, in my mind I had recycled the events that led to our parting and in my foolishness I had blamed you. I bear the responsibility now, you were a girl in love; I was a man riddled by doubts; doubts that were strong enough to stop me from fighting for you like the rare gem that you were. I remember that day when you said "Momoh, we need to talk. A young doctor has come to work with my dad and my parents want me to be with him. I had felt like something heavy had been placed on my head. The first day I met you, you were seven but you had grown to be a nineteen year old beauty about to enter university. I was a twenty-one year old man with a WASSCE result but my mum had not been able to afford my university fees for the second year in a row. How would I compete with a doctor? I had thought. I remember you had held my hand and said, "Please Momoh, come and see my parents. We cannot hide forever". I did not; I groped like a fool. What I should have done was to put my arms around you and reassure you of my love. I should have walked boldly with you to your house and faced your father. Instead, I had pushed you away and asked you in fright, "Egertina, what is this doctor's name?" You had hesitated before answering "Prince Peacock". The name had irritated me then, simply because you were a princess but I was no prince. It was blatantly clear. "You should be happy, Egertina George, you have a prince now. Just go away and let me be, marry him and make your parents happy," I had snapped. I remember that you had burst into tears. You had cried a long time before you left. I was such a fool to let you leave. Egertina, it is too little and way too late, but I want you to know that I am sorry. I was just afraid you would see the truth that I have always known. The truth that you have always been too good for me. I had stayed in the woods after you left, wrapped up in my misery. It was later in the evening that

I was able to make my way home. What I saw when I got home was a sight that still hurts me. I had seen my mother kneeling down in front of your dad. She was crying and pleading with him while the other tenants looked on. He had raised his hand and struck my mum in the face. I was going to pounce on him and beat him senselessly but I was restrained by the fact that he was your father. I had walked up to him and calmly said, "If you touch my mother again I would make you regret it". He had turned towards me and furiously muttered, "My daughter came home in tears to tell us she wants to marry you. A filthy, wretched boy with no future. Is it my money you want? Is that why you are deceiving my daughter?" I had looked at him as he raged, face barely recognizable. Equally enraged, I had said to him the three words which contained all the hope in my world. "Egertina loves me". He hit me then, in the face and for a moment, I had seen darkness; I had felt my nose bleed. My Mama's sobbing grew louder. Then he was gone, into his car and out of our compound. I had lifted my mother up and taken her indoors. There we had soothed our pains.

My mother spoke to me that night. I remember her calling my name softly, "Momoh you need to forget this girl. You are worlds apart and you can never be together. Concentrate on making something good of yourself and you will see... girls would come running". I had known that was the last of her advice I would heed and I had wept bitterly. "Mama," I had said helplessly, "I love her." Though bitter, she had smiled and cuddling me, had said, "I know my son, but you would always love another". Fool that I was, I had believed her.

You came to me that night, Egertina. It was after Mama had slept. You had knocked on my door and I had gone outside to find you frozen in the moon light. Your eyes were red and swollen. As soon as you saw me, you had flung your arms around me and muttered desperately, "I stole some money, let us run away together, my love." At the time, I earnestly had believed I was doing the right thing when I pushed you away and ranted out, "Egertina, go home and marry your prince. I am not going anywhere with you. I am just tired of you and your family. Please leave me alone". You immediately had burst into tears and had gone away. What can I say now; "I am so sorry, Egertina".

The next morning, I had woken up and realized I had made a mistake. I didn't know what made me come to my senses but I suddenly did. I had walked out of my house on to your doorsteps and knocked at your door. An elderly woman had answered me and without hesitation or fear, I had asked for you. There my world had finally collapsed. *"Madam Egertina don go Freetown for marry Mr. Peacock,"* the woman had said. It was like my soul had been crushed.

Egertina, that was how that love had ended. It was better I was not around when you came back, for I would not have been able to stand seeing you with another man and knowing, with all certainty, that my Egertina was now somebody else's. I later won D.V and left Kenema with my mother to start a new life in America. I am happy I was able to give my mother a better life. I am grateful she was able to see her son a success. Now, I am back to bury her; to give her a final resting place in her own land. Egertina, I devoted myself to work and I made something of myself. You will be proud of me. Like Mama had said, girls have come running. But none of them are you, Egertina. None of their eyes sparkle the way yours do.

So I must end this letter; this final letter to you, my beloved.

My love for you knows no time, knows no place, and has no end.

I am yours,
Momoh.

Momoh looked at the hospital before him. It was his. Part of his investment plan for his country and he would be meeting his staff today. An enthusiastic secretary met him at the door. "Good afternoon, sir. It is time to meet your staff," she said smiling. Momoh followed her and as they climbed the steps, the secretary briefed him.

"First, we were able to engage the services of a renowned Cardiologist, her name is Dr. George. In fact, here she is".

She said no more, for both Momoh's and the lady's face had gone pale. They stared at each other in total shock. Finally, the man found his voice.

"Hello Egertina".

The lady was still in oblivion and so could not answer. The man then turned to the perplexed secretary and said, "Please excuse us for a moment". The secretary scurried out, happy to escape the awkward situation.

Momoh had countless questions in his mind.

"Why are you Dr. George? I thought you got married".

The lady, still in daze, just shook her head.

"I never married, Momoh. I ran away on my wedding day to look for you but you had gone. You did not even leave a message. I had to move on, Momoh. You had forgotten about me," the lady finally found herself saying. Momoh, now spellbound, watched the lady, his Egertina, blink back tears and he felt ashamed once again, and guilty he had hurt her. She spoke then,

"I had no idea you owned this place. Anyways, let me get back to work". She turned her back and he grabbed her and forced her to face him.

"Have dinner with me, sweet Egertina, my love, please do".

She hesitated and forgetting her vow, she said,

"I will, Momoh".

In the evening, the secretary saw them walking down the stairs, their voices were happy and they played childishly. When they reached her, they just went by, without heeding her, for they had eyes only for each other. They spoke of a brighter future.

This companionship I just witnessed must be the result of true love and true love does not die, the secretary thought, smiled and found her way into the interior of the building.

Joan Adama Kainessie

Submission

I woke up one afternoon and saw my mother, Jatu, sitting in the back yard, gazing at a distance…lost. She could not even notice my presence when I walked and stood beside her. I could trace the beauty that used to be on her face before our existence, with its dimples and beauty mark that rested on the top right of her lips. A beauty now covered with wrinkles. The dimples had left a hole on each jaw making her look toothless and the colour of her eyes was being washed away with tears, leaving it with shades of grey. "Mama!" I called. She slanted toward me and held my hands. Then I asked her, "Does submission go with pain?" She paused, smiled at me and answered, "Nooo!" She then tapped my legs and I stared into her eyes. "It goes with love and blessed children," she again said softly, looking into my eyes with the same air of tenderness. I lived with this pain, witnessing my father abuse and kill the beauty on my mother's face—torturing her soul with words and actions—without laying a finger on her, for Papa's words were strong and could kill a cat. He spent few hours a day in the house; those moments he spent finding meaningless faults to rage hell, and then he would leave for unknown destinations only to return at odd hours knocking. My mother, his night security guard, would scamper about to open and serve him. That was routine. Sometimes, I could hear Mama cry and talk to him, asking him salient questions of what went wrong, but he never responded. This sadness was a shadow in my mind and was killing me inside. Her skin wrinkled and her skeleton projected, displaying every curve and edge. I could see the pain in her eyes while struggling to provide our needs; working tirelessly in her back yard garden and also helping our neighbours to harvest and clear their farms so she would be given some crops or food to bring home. One day, as we talked, I said to her, "You could have been better off being single than married". "Shhhhhh!" she interrupted, "Don't say that! Someday, you'll understand it all. It's a commandment," Mama said. I looked into her teary eyes, shocked.They seemed to tell many gory stories of matrimony. So I raised my brows and, for some reason, focussed on her face. My gaze beamed at her wrinkles but she avoided my stare and flipped through series of pages from the Bible and read, "Husband, love your Wife. Wife, be submissive." It was then I knew what submission really meant—it was to her, an exchange for love—and that I had misunderstood, through and through. Brainwashed by religious tradition, Mama had remained detrimentally submissive albeit she was never loved or cared for. She submitted to his wrath, anger and abusive torture. I looked into her eyes, angered by her being so tolerant to such smitten treatments and she said to me, "My daughter, be patient. We'll one day get through this". I looked at her again, this time with slight irritation, and nodded in doubt. "How can anything good come out of such servitude?" I mused. Her courage, I admired though—she was a strong woman!

One day, I rushed home, from school, running to meet her smiles and hugs as she usually had and I saw a crowd from the village and beyond crying and singing. As I came closer, people shook their heads and some women, in grief, held me close and led me to my father who was seated drowned with tears, telling people how precious his wife was to him. I was muted to hear his words. I coldly walked towards the door and, in the middle of our parlour, I saw her lying and smiling in the white silk she was wrapped in. This time, she was not able to hug me and ask me questions about school. In that silk wrapper, her beauty still shone. She glowed and looked much younger, maintaining that smile of peace. My mother died a submissive wife. The drums beat slowly while the villagers from Koya sang and clapped. My siblings were smeared with white cam wood powder; the native boys from Kuwama took the corpse out to the centre of the court while relatives, friends and the entire neighbourhood circled around her remains, paying their last respect. The ceremony began. My siblings, Marie and Haja, were each asked to pass by the corpse three times so as to create darkness between them and the dead. And now it was Papa's turn to pay his last respect to his wife, our mother. His feet were too weak to walk so his brothers held him up and helped him walk toward the corpse. He opened his mouth, looked at me and attempted to speak but nothing came out of his mouth. Papa stood by his wife. He stretched his hands toward the corpse but he could not touch it. After performing all the traditional rites, it was time for the burial procession to commence. Since my father was a devout Muslim, the religious rites were done in the Islamic way. Men were separated from women and the procession moved toward the cemetery; women stayed home to cook and serve. I stood by the door as they walked away with her, my mother, speechless. Our family members stayed with us for a while and then left in batches till they were all gone. When all was over, a silence broke in the house. Papa wanted to initiate something but he did not know where to begin. His eye could not reach mine as he kept it down constantly. Sometimes, he fought to keep eye contact with me but he could not. For those few days, he tried to stay home. He mourned his wife and, for once, he took great care of us. He and his younger brother did the cooking and laundering while I took care of Haja and Marie. As time went on, Papa became sick and once more we faced hardship. His health got bad by the day and he was not able to take care of our needs.

I ended up leaving school for Mama's garden to educate my sisters and feed the home while Uncle Rahman stayed home to look after Papa. Sometimes, I barely sold anything, so I would have to go to the bush, find wild yams, *maggie* leaves and palm kennel nuts to survive. Haja, my youngest sister, always cried, for she disliked bush yam and that made me to worry as I would have to go and look for potatoes from the garden for her. One evening, as I was about to retire from work, Papa called me for the first time in five years. "Ada," he cried, "I'm sorry. I know I wronged your mother and you all. I was not able to ask for her forgiveness but now I can ask for yours," he wailed. I was drowning in tears as he spoke, for I had forgiven him already. He raised his head and looked at me. I was sitting on his lap, helping to wipe his tears. "Papa," I called, "I have forgiven you shortly after Mama's funeral. And I have waited long enough for a day like this. You need not to explain further," I assured him, "We are your children and we love you. All you should do is to ask for God's forgiveness, for he is a forgiving God". We embraced and sobbed profusely.

After that day, Papa's health deteriorated and we could not afford to take him for medical treatment until one day when Pa Morlie's son, who came to visit from the city, visited our house with his parents asking for Marie's hand in marriage. By then, she had passed her WASSC Examinations and we were thinking about her learning some trade first. He was just on time when, during the conversation, Papa fainted. They rushed him to his car and took him to the village clinic. When we got home later in the day, we tried explaining to Alpha how badly we wanted Marie to be educated and he promised to foot her university bills and, he also helped with Papa's medications in the city. He equally took care of Haja and I who stayed in the village. After four years, Marie graduated and Alpha came back home with her. He came with his relatives and asked again for Marie's hand in marriage. They told us they were now ready to do the traditional wedding. Papa had no option but to accept the family's proposal as Alpha had proved himself a good in-law. Arrangements were made; people, from the city and beyond our village, were invited. At the ceremony, Papa asked for a moment of silence for his wife. After which, the ceremony continued—people ate and drank, drums were played and a professional flute player came in and played tunes that told stories. The elders listened, smiled and cheered him up. That evening, the groom took his bride to his father's village-house and as tradition demanded, the village women stood outside and waited in anticipation. After moments of silence, the door screeched and the groom walked out. He held a bundle of white cloth with fresh blood on it. This sent the village women clapping. They danced and celebrated. The following day, the bride and groom visited Papa to inform him about their departure to the city and also to ask for Haja to join them so that she could be able to further her schooling there. Papa was happy and he blessed them. As they left, I held Papa's hand. I noticed his excitement as we walked into the house. He could not stop telling me how happy he was and he prayed to God for me. Years passed by and Alpha and Marie came home to announce their joy—Marie's pregnancy. Papa was excited about the news of his first grandchild and he immediately started giving it boyish names. We all laughed at the strangeness of the names: *Nyakeh*, *Mukeh*, and a host of other traditional names. "How would you tell the baby will be a boy?" I asked laughing. "I could see it from her belly shape," he rejoined with a broad grin. More things happened. Our house was renovated by Alpha and we lived comfortably in it. Marie gave birth to a bouncing baby boy as Papa had hoped. He was named Mukeh. Alpha built a new apartment in the city and he asked his family and our family to go and live with them so that I could help Marie with the kids and Papa could see his grandchildren grow. Marie gave birth to a second and a third child and Papa enjoyed playing with his grandchildren. On to the day I watched him take his last breath on my lap, Papa never ceased to tell me stories about my childhood.

Mohamed Gibril Sesay

Chronicle of a Birth Foretold

Maseray's pregnancy passed the nine months' mark, passed ten months, eleven months...twenty months. Her tribulation raged within like waves vexed by the gravitational madness of the moon, which as you know, is also called the lunatic light. Doctors and nurses at the clinic could not fathom this mystery. A medicine-man did. But telling Maseray and her husband, KothYaro was not part of his earthly destiny... was not part of the medicine-man's earthly destiny to tell his clients about their child's bigger-than-ordinary head getting stuck at the birth-way... Pain upon pain, Maseray flung her legs at opposite ends of the stained walls of the labour ward, cursing her husband for not sharing the pain with her, as he had done with the pleasure that was the source of this agony. But an old woman did warn her, "Maseray, it's not good for a pregnant woman to wash in the open spaces of the night." She did not heed the advice. She was one of the post-moderns. *Everything is a myth.* Even herself.

"Well, at least, put charcoal in the water."

She laughed the old woman off. But the old woman had hardly left when a spirit, also called *krifi,* slicked through her unprotected vulva and merged its identity with that of the fetus.

Outside the labour ward, KothYaro's mother, who loathed what she called the free life of her daughter-in-law, was telling relatives, "Let her confess her wrong doings, let her do it."

KothYaro was pouring money like rain on nurses prescribing this and that.

But the head still stuck.

"Let her confess her infidelities," KothYaro's mother was truly convinced about her daughter-in-law's wrong doings, "If she doesn't tell us about her infidelities, she will not give birth."

The head still stuck. The doctor could see the scalp of the boy at the edge of the vagina, but that was it, it was not moving out...

"Sure," said KothYaro's mother, "this Maseray must have been up to some games against my son. For how could she claim to be true to my son when she never bothered to get me hot water to bathe, or give me the meals' choicest parts, or show me my meals with respect? No, she never knelt down to give me water, never waited on me when eating; always coming and going, coming and going... never bothered to say goodbye or tell me where she was going... And my son's such a fool. But he was not like that before he married this woman... Sure, this woman must have turned my son's heart inside-out by putting the last little jot of her shit in my son's food; she must have given my son the dirty water left from the laundering of her dirty pubic knickers. Yes, I refused to eat the food she had carelessly thrown at me as she hurried to only God knows where. How could I eat that? I'm not a dog. No. I'm her mother-in-law, the mother of her husband, my own true son; no other person gave birth to him for me, so she should respect me more than she does her husband, for if I hadn't given birth to KothYaro, would she have seen him? If I hadn't cared for him more than I cared for my own body...

When KothYaro came back home he had asked why I hadn't eaten.

'Look KothYaro,' I had told him, 'I'm not a dog who gladly eats meals thrown at it.'

'She threw the food at you?' he had asked.

'Ask her.'

'Where is she?'

'EeeKothYaro, so you don't know where your wife is?'

'I was not in when she went out... Maybe she had gone to...'

'Hmm! Son, who married who?'

'Why Mama, we married ourselves...'

The head was slowly tearing its way through the birth-way. A nurse, no gloves, was impatiently trying to open Maseray with one hand and gyrating her backside with the other.

"Bring forty thousand," a nurse with a backside like a cock's ordered the impatient KothYaro.

"Here."

She grabbed it like armed robbers do, went into a room, hurriedly came out with a dark bottle containing nothing, passed it down KothYaro's trousers and went into the suffer-ward.

'...You married yourselves? Well done son... But who... who is the boss here... I mean who controls this house?'

'Eee Mama, what type of question is that?'

'I what to know, I really want to know...your wife is too free...too out of control...look KothYaro, if you want your woman to be faithful to you, be hard, a man must be hard."

The head reached the edge of the birth-way. But a rough scar at the upper end of the gateway to the world was blocking its final thrust to a new mode of existence. Time was running out... The medicine-man had foreseen the child being born before the mid-afternoon prayers... And at yonder Mosque, the muezzin was climbing up the minaret. It was then that Yeanor invaded KothYaro's memory... "I told you, you will pay for it, that I'll make you know that I haven't forgotten my roots."

"But Yeanor, Yeanor please," KothYaro gasped after the shadow and bumped into his mother.

"What's wrong with you KothYaro?" his mother asked.

"She was here, I saw her," he answered.

"Who was here? Who did you see?"

"Yeanor, Yeanor's ghost, she said she is making me pay for dumping her"

"Yeanor, yes Yeanor… the real daughter-in-law that you kicked out for this false one called Maseray. Ah KothYaro, you wronged Yeanor. You destroyed her schooling; you impregnated her out of school. But no, you never looked back to that… You kicked her out for Maseray. You met this wayward Maseray in a rum-bar, brought her home and ordered Yeanor out of the matrimonial bed. Yeanor refused. So you beat her up. You and newfound love, Maseray, you beat her up…"

The muezzin was calling believers for the mid-afternoon prayer. The head was getting desperate… It must get out during this time; that was what the medicine-man had foreseen…Next to the writhing Maseray, another woman was giving successful birth to another boy for whom this as yet unborn child, whose head still stuck, would be severely beaten, for it was said:

"Eighteen years hence, you will strip your mother naked and stab her belly and then give your father the severest of beatings. And when the trial judge shall ask you why, you will reply, 'Mother disgraced me by screwing politicians to feed and clothe the family and for silently bowing his head to that, I could've killed father had neighbours not overpowered me'…"

But that was not the only time the prescience of this *krifi* child landed him in trouble. The other time he was flogged by inmates of a house he had predicted would be ablaze in about a month's time. Ah, you remember the other time he told us about the approach of difficult times for the nation. Times that would be rougher than where chickens sleep... times when the pregnant would give premature birth on the fleeing road; when beasts shall devour the ill-born and the ill-dead; about how three minutes' old mothers would be fucked by hard hearted men with guns; about barbaric slaughtering and kidnappings and savage rapes...about how even the blind would toddle on stones and swamps in blind dreams of safety...and about how even words would die from the fatigue of carrying more sorrowing accounts than they were made for... Ah, you remember when he told us about diamonds smeared with blood; gold mixed with human grit, about peasants forced to tote bags of looted coffee and cocoa for hundreds of miles; about the amputation of the hands of voters; about the woman forced to suckle the hacked off head of her son; about the merchants of death; the suppliers of arms from the fastnesses of Charlemagne...And about that seaman he said water would kill? The man stopped going to sea... But then he choked on a teaspoon of water and died. The children loved him. Not so, the adults? The *krifi* child frightened them with his hidden knowledge. He told them about themselves in public... joined those stories, which they would want to keep apart... presented the fullness of their inherent contradiction in public. About what they did under the cloak of God, under the cover of night.

And especially so the greedy, the stingy, the rock-hearted, those who would not give him money to give his little friends. These, he told only the evil sides of their past, present and future. About how they fucked their sisters-in-law and ate monies meant for the dead.

Thus, the good children wept and the bad adults rejoiced when the big headed child was eaten up by a mangy cat whose head alone was twice its size.

"It's good that he should die this way... this child always has evil words in his mouth," the old man said.

All that happened years after the *Krifi* child's head got stuck at the birth-way, peeling away Maseray's scars of womanhood. Blood upon blood. The *krifi* child's desperation to get out as had been foreseen by the medicine-man made him thrash his feet all over the insides of Maseray in order to gain momentum, in order to develop escape velocity. Maseray writhed in dire dolour, the dolour of death's dagger digging deeper until she died.

KothYaro blamed the newly-born child for Maseray's death, and for days he would sing thus of his wife:

Me soul 'member her smiles
Sole balms on sharp miles

Me soul feel her bead
In the loneliness of her bed

Me soul mourn her groin
Me soul groan

Me soul see the dream drown
Me soul since then is down

Listen big headed son
Listen o! You death-bringing person
Let me tell you 'bout
The woman you killed at your birth

But the big headed boy, not yet even two months, shocked KothYaro with a reply:

"No, I did not kill Maseray. I was a spirit desirous of becoming a human. I searched and searched for passage ways onto the human world. I had already given up when one hot night I found Maseray washing in the open spaces of the night and zoomed into her unprotected vulva. It was good that I did, for the fetus was already disintegrating, already sliding down the path its father's semen had come through to fertilize its mother's egg. That fetus, my dear KothYaro, could have become a casualty of Maseray's monthly ovular flux. Do you know how many billions of fertilized eggs don't make it to full human-hood? How many trillions of potential humans become casualties of the path? That the paths of life are strewn with thorns of death? Let me tell you, casualties never end, only reminisces make them bearable. But even remembering is an art; you've got to have in them the flair, or else it becomes the tumbril that carries you to the ultimate agony.

Casualties never end... Whilst we were yet spermatozoa, swinging on scrotal vines, others were already humans in this world, swinging from one event to another. Some never made it; they were too heavy for the aroused ecstasies of the father to swing them out. The scrotum became their tomb; casualties of the struggle of life, for life... won't you hallow them? Others got out but not in, they could not slide up the vulva, the path of Eve, of life as we know it. Cadavers of semen washed off at the next cleansing of the loins. These sperms never developed skeletons; so they never became fossilized. Lost forever? Perhaps. Yes, only dinosaurs leave fossils, only tyrants leave records for fine treatment at the museums of this and that history. That we may tremble. But what about the grass they trampled upon? What about the ferns those terrible lizards of yore crushed? Science tells us that those crushed grass rot down there, become dark oil sucked up to lubricate this wicked nowdom, crushed in life and death. Billions of events sprout out of every arousal of the world, but the vast majority never makes it to the memories of humankind. Why? Why is it that the vast majority never becomes information for humankind? Why is it that so many stories never made it? Casualties never end, that we may be, they were wiped out. Every now and then, billions of semen, billions of these wee pendulous human possibilities bombard the walls of ova in order to increase their odds of becoming human. But when only one spermatozoon gets into the ovum…Nuances! Nuances! Nuances! Sometimes two spermatozoa simultaneously enter two ova and we have non-identical zygotes. But for the unsuccessful millions, the result is always the same: the emergent zygote(s) play(s) the victor and through secretion of chemical repellents scare(s) off the unsuccessful desperados. What else, they've lost their chance to become higher possibilities for human existence. Eons old efforts poured on a hope whose realization eludes them at the crucial moment. So they beat off a retreat (the story of their efforts imprinted in their disintegration). Aluta continua—the struggle continues.

Nuances! Nuances! Sometimes, this victor, this mingling, this murderous zygote, regrets being alone. So it divides into two and we have identical zygotes. Perchance one fails to make it to the human realm, the other will. Nuances never end! Sometimes the self-hacking is incomplete… Nuances! Nuances! Other times, the zygotes hug each other, fuse their wee essences (or one tries to swallow the other, but the other resists; one cannot swallow; the other cannot be swallowed). They are given birth to, joined to each other; sometimes by the heads, or chests. What should we make of this, this thorn pricking our will to definitional clarity, this fuzziness; a human *krifi* with two heads and eight arms. Casualties never end, for we kill them off. Every human is but a lucky actualization of a possibility that contended with a million other possibilities, each of which could have occupied the space and time that you are now occupying. Won't you say thanks? But to whom? To which God or non-God? That's what divides. Nuances! Nuances! Sometimes some genes run berserk; so unruly, they play not by the rules of the code. And behold, another imperfection is groomed for the human realm. But who has not got nuances within? Or without? Who is it that dares tell us they are perfect humans in all their genes, all their cells, all their organs, in all their dispositions, in all their behaviour? But too many nuances wreck too many zygotes. Many fetuses never make it, too slippery they glue themselves to the warm tender sustenance of the uterus. So unlucky, so unlucky. So they slide down... But hey, sometimes the zygote becomes an ectopic rebel, it takes a stance where it should not, it takes a stance in the fallopian tube, and we have ectopic pregnancies, life threatening. But most times the zygote could not take that stance. They miss the carriage of life and slide down the path. Some slide down without notice, causing no grief. Others go down with tragic displays, oozing blood, destroying tissues, damaging fallopian tubes, causing great pains to mothers.

That could have been the fate of the fetus that was in Maseray had I not energized it, given it stickiness, the will to resist the ovular flux, the will to hope for higher state of existence... It was not an easy fight. I fused my spirit with a fetus that had not wanted to become human, a fetus that had too many rioting genes and cells, a fetus that wanted to die, and be flushed out, or if it could not be flushed out, that did not mind dying with Maseray. I wrestled with it, giving

Maseray too many jolts and pain as her stomach became a battle ground between a will to die and a will to live. I won the fight, and was ready to move out when it was time to be born. But, unexpectedly, my head got stuck at the birth canal of Maseray. And it had been foretold that I should get out before the-mid afternoon prayer or else greater tragedy would come to pass."

And at yonder Mosque, the muezzin was climbing the minaret to call the faithful unto prayers.

Mohamed Sheriff

Sori Clever

Anytime I witness someone getting drunk, I remember the story of the widow and the drunkard. Heard it told in a bar a long time ago, but it stuck so fast in my mind, it's as if I were there to see how it all happened. How the drunkard in some way fell in love with the widow and how the widow too loved him in her own way. How she once told him if he stopped drinking, she'd agree to marry him and he had asked if she meant that and she had said 'yes' and he had broken down and cried. But all that is not the fascinating part of their story— it was after that that the unforgettable thing happened. No, no, not one of those dark haunting stories—a funny story, really.

The widow, Musu Kamara, a provision stall owner, was still young and beautiful, with two lovely daughters; the drunkard, Sori, can't remember the surname, was an unemployed, middle-aged man, fighting chronic alcoholism. Quite a resourceful fellow, Sori was. Well, resourceful, really, at only one thing: he could charm even a miser into buying him a drink. He was fondly called Sori Clever. Story goes of how he got a heavy drinking miser, a certain Elvis, into buying him not one but two whole bottles of beer. To this day, Elvis, now an old drunk, I hear, continues to moan and at the same time marvel at how Sori made him part with two bottles of beer. He swore he was bewitched by the drunk.

Sori was once a protective guard at the Customs Department at the International Seaport where he had enriched himself as a member of a port syndicate that helped importers evade custom duties. A spendthrift he was, popular for his open-handedness at bars and nightclubs, starting sunup on Fridays till almost sundown on Mondays. He was always badgered by poor neighbours, friends and relatives whom he would help out of financial difficulties. Musu was a beneficiary of his generosity, putting her in business as a provision stall owner even though she had rejected his amorous advances over a dozen times. Before that, she hawked fruits on her head from place to place, rain or shine.

Sorie's fortune took a plunge when he was jailed for corruption and he lost everything he had to the state. Many believed he was just a victim of the collateral damage caused by the crash of the man in the highest seat at the port management. Being one of the big man's sidekicks, running his shady, subterranean errands, including customs duty related fraudulent transactions; he was swept along during the house cleaning exercise aimed at his boss who had fallen foul of the boss of all bosses, the boss who occupied the highest seat of state. Some say Sori's boss was a secret supporter of the arch political rival of Big Boss. Some say Sori's boss "held Big Boss's hand underwater", which means he double-crossed Big Boss in a deal. Whatever the truth, no one believed Sori's boss went down because of his dirty deals. If that were the case, very few people would have escaped the big broom that swept Sori and his boss. An old friend of my father used to say that in this country it's pretty easy to nail big men in big offices for corruption. "Most live well above their official income," he would argue when challenged. "Where are they getting the extra money?"

"Everyone lives above their income in this country," father, who loves a good argument, would say. "And without being in debt—a real miracle."

"When poor folks like us live above our income, that's a miracle… but when big men do, well, we all know what that is," he would end sarcastically.

Those were the many reasons given as to why Sori, his boss and eight others in their syndicate were fired, made to give up much of their ill-gotten wealth and serve various jail terms. After three years he was released from prison, a drunkard, penniless, homeless and friendless. All his friends turned their backs on him, except Musu, whose husband had just died. She gave him a room in her apartment and fed him two times a day. For this, Sori was grateful but he wanted money to drink. That, unfortunately, didn't come by easily. What little he got he spent on cheap, strong drink. His usual haunt was the *Red Hot Spot Bar* where he was once treated as a VIP. Once a talented stage actor, he would go to the bar to charm customers and perform all kinds of antics to get a drink. The reason he was called Sori Clever, but when he got more aggressive in his demand, harassing customers for liquor, making a nuisance of himself and embarrassing the management, he was barred from going to the *Red Hot Spot Bar*. Not daunted by that, he started lurking behind Musu's stall which was directly opposite the short drive leading to the *Red Hot Spot Bar* just across the road, hoping to sweet talk some old friend into giving him money to buy drink. This closeness to Musu rekindled his attraction for her. He felt love in his heart for her once again.

"Now that your husband is dead, will you marry me? I know I'm a useless drunk now, but remember what I used to be. All is not lost, Musu".

"If you stop drinking, even if you are jobless, I'll marry you," she responded, and she meant it. She had always been fond of him; she could very well be in love with him and her daughters would have a father at home once again.

"Do you mean that?"

"Yes I do, Sori ."

Sorie was so moved that he wept. "I give you my word, Musu. I'll never touch liquor again."

It was easier said than done. He would keep away from booze for three or four days and then drink himself to oblivion, apologise to Musu for the relapse, renew his promise, abstain for another couple of days, and then go back to drinking again. He could not help it.

Late one evening, after a week of abstinence, perhaps the longest since his first promise, Sori was sitting by Musu, just behind her stall, when they saw a turbaned youth in an ankle-length coat over a kaftan walking down the drive towards the *Red Hot Spot Bar.*

"What on earth is he going there for?" Musu asked.

"He is a member of MADAACC, *Movement against Drug Abuse and Alcohol Consumption and Crime*, a religious youth group whose members go around bars and smoking joints preaching God's message against alcohol, drug and crime."

"Are they not inviting trouble from drug addicts and criminals?" Musu asked.

"They are also tough and full of religious zeal, but generally peaceful. Usually they go in group and keep their distance," Sori explained.

"But that one has come all by himself and he's certainly not keeping his distance," Musu said, shaking her head.

That was long before 9/11, El Shabab, BokoHaram or ISIS. Muslims and Islam were not so feared and hated in the West then. Now, a group like MADAACC would have raised a storm in Western diplomatic circles within the country. There would have been a visit to our Internal Affairs Ministry by the heads of mission of the US and her Western allies. Back then, their activities caused only few eye lashes to flutter and some detached amusement.

They could see the turbaned youth outside the bar, preaching to the amused customers. Then suddenly, two waiters burst out of the bar, rushed at the young man, grabbed him and pinned both his hands behind his back. The proprietor, a hefty man, emerged smiling mischievously, a bottle of cold beer held in his left hand. He advanced slowly towards the captive preacher.

"Oh God, they are going to force him to drink the liquor," Musu cried from behind her stall.

Realizing what was about to happen to him, the preacher broke free from his captors and bolted up the drive to the main road, moving surprisingly fast for a man in long coat and Kaftan.

"The next time you come here, I'll lock you in the bar until the next morning," the proprietor yelled after him.

Sorie was silent and thoughtful for a while after that incident. "Musu," he said at length, "Do you know that I've not touched liquor for a whole week now?"

"Yes I do," she answered smiling.

"I want to go to my village and spend a couple of weeks there away from temptation."

Musu looked hard at him and seeing that he was serious, whispered, "I'll miss you but I think it's a good idea."

He left in the afternoon of the following day. Late that night, as Musu was packing her goods into her boxes to retire for the day, she held her breath when the light of a passing vehicle picked up a turbaned figure in a long coat standing at the junction of the drive leading to the bar. His face was all wrapped up like a Tuareg, leaving a small opening for his eyes.

This fellow is daring, she thought, as the man walked down the drive. "Alone again today, after that narrow escape yesterday. He is asking for whatever happens to him." Musu headed home still thinking about the preacher.

She came to her stall the following morning at ten and was surprised at the scene of commotion that greeted her outside the *Red Hot Spot*. Some thirty turbaned members of MADAACC in long coats were outside the bar holding long sticks as weapons, chanting religious slogans and hurling threats at the proprietor who looked very much cowed. He had carried out his threat and locked up the MADAACC member whom Musu had seen going down the drive the previous night. Somehow, word had reached MADAACC and now it appeared as if they were going to burn down the bar. A large crowd of on-lookers had gathered. Musu joined them.

The proprietor was in a dilemma. If he opened the door he would be in trouble; if he stalled, they would force their way in and he would be in big trouble.

"We are going to give you ten counts to open that door, or else no one, not even the police will stop us from breaking in," a hefty youth in front threatened. He was wielding the biggest stick, his goatee beard, long and unkempt. "After ten counts..."

"One, two, three," began the MADAACC boys in unison.

The proprietor fished out his keys from his pocket and opened the door. Ten MADAACC boys brushed past him and entered the bar. A sudden hush fell over the place. The tension in the atmosphere was electric. From where she stood in the crowd, Musu could see the proprietor sweating profusely and trembling with fear. She wished Sori were there to see his enemy, who had barred him from the *Red Hot Spot*, cowed and sweating. After what seemed like ages, the MADAACC boys came out. In front of them was the man they had come to set free. Musu watched him in dismay. His face was no longer wrapped up, nor was the turban on his head. He was swaying unsteadily in drunken stupor with a bottle of beer in each hand, one each in the side pockets of his long coat and another forced into the breast pocket of his kaftan. He raised both bottles and waved them at the crowd which exploded into uproarious shouts and laughter. Then, in unison, they started clapping and chanting "Sori clever Sori clever!" It was Sori alright. Musu turned her back on them and walked away, not knowing whether to laugh or to cry.

A Diary in the Head of a Street Child Beggar

I'm standing in a crowded street in the middle of Freetown. No food since morning and it's past two o'clock. The heat and hunger make my head spin. Life is tough for a displaced, especially if you're a ten-year-old orphan. Food rations are few and far between. So we beg sometimes. But even begging can be tough and painful. Like today.

A lady comes. She looks kind. Maybe she'll give me something. "Good morning ma'. I'm begging for God. He'll bless you. Give me something to eat. Grandma is ill. She has no food. God will bless you." She has gone! Not even a glance. That's how most behave. It's as if they're ashamed when we beg them. Maybe it's because we look so dirty and are smelly sometimes. Or maybe we may give them disease. This reminds me of Grandma. She's got tuberculosis. That's what Pa Usu says. She coughs a lot. Sometimes there's blood. She's very weak these days. She has no more strength even to go to hospital. That's why I beg more often now. Our neighbours, Pa Usu's family, in the other tent, say Grandma is dying. I'm worried. I'll have no one. Me and Grandma were made to watch as our whole family burn inside our house. Their screams wake me up some nights.

Here comes another lady. I may be lucky this time. I walk towards her. She gives me a severe look. I walk past. She reminds me of another I begged from the other day. "Out of my sight," she says. "Did I kill your parents? Idle child! Your parents just leave you to roam the street like a stray dog," she continues and walks away. How could she be so cruel? She didn't know me. I have only Grandma. Life is cruel. But all this is better than being attacked by rebels or being captured by them. We were made captive for one week—me and Grandma. They gave me some strange powder to take. It made my head reel. They tried to teach me how to shoot. Fortunately, we were rescued by *ECOMOG* before I was sent on a mission. Thank God they've signed a peace agreement. The sound of a gun sends the weakness of fear down the back of my legs. Even the explosion of a tyre...or a door banging...if there is anymore fighting...I'll just die.

I was worried. Grandma told me the grey bearded rebel leader had a hidden plan. What did he want then? Grandma also said he had been offered everything to make him happy and stop fighting. "But *UNAMSIL* will take care of him," she had said. *UNAMSIL,* the peace keepers. They were great people, the *UNAMSIL*. I had admired them in their big military trucks and non-military jeeps, especially the jeeps— sleek and shiny. "Will I ever ride one?" A big boy in our camp, one of Pa Usu's sons, had told me they were all well- off—the *UNAMSIL* people. I had believed him. I had wished to be a *UNAMSIL* when I grew up—no, an *ECOMOG*. "*UNAMSIL* were the elder brothers of ECOMOG," Grandma had told me. "But ECOMOG were braver," Grandma had said. She had believed all dead Nigerian and *ECOMOG* soldiers would go to Heaven. I want to go to heaven too with Grandma. Heaven is beautiful. No hunger, no war, no rebels. There is a lot of bread with milk and honey, fresh fruits and vegetables. O, the thought of them makes my stomach rumble. And evergreen shade-trees, cool spring water and peace. I wish God will take me and Grandma to Heaven. I must go now. I'm feeling dizzy. No luck today, Grandma. I'm also not well. I cough a lot too. Not like Grandma, but I cough too. And it's painful. Also, I sweat a lot at night. Everything gets wet—blanket, clothes...I feel very uncomfortable...the weakness is getting worse. It's daylight but the place is getting dark. I can't see clearly...I think I'm falling. I hear a distant voice shouting...

I'm sure I fainted. Now I'm conscious of voices, but I can't open my eyes.

"Poor child," a voice cries, he's vomited so much blood. "It must be tuberculosis," another voice says.

Now I can smell the blood. Taste it. I can feel it all over my mouth and neck.

"Can't someone pick him up and take him to the hospital?" a voice says.

"Why don't you do it?" another says angrily.

"Too risky. Tuberculosis is infectious," says yet another voice.

"He's far gone, he's going to die," a strong male voice says.

I think I'm losing consciousness again... too many voices, too many footsteps, moving back and forth...I... It's all clear to me now. I'm dying. No doubt about that...

Moses Kainwo

Wheelbarrow Man

Back in the day, Bimbahun and intelligence were synonymous. Fanta recalled how he used to top their class in one of the best secondary schools in the country. His fame spread after correcting Mr. Penman, an American working with Peace Corps. One Friday afternoon, Mr. Penman had asked the Form Four students to solve a math problem as homework for the weekend. On Monday morning, Mr. Penman had taken the big ruler and drawn the diagram of a rhombus on the chalkboard. He then asked the class to go to the chalkboard and solve the problem. One after the other, they had failed. Finally, Mr. Penman decided to solve the problem as it was already time for lunch and the other pupils from the other classes had already crowded at the windows. Mr. Penman started scribbling and when it was obvious he could not solve the problem, Bimbahun had volunteered to go to the chalkboard.

"First of all, the diagram is wrong!" Bimbahun said with confidence.

"How do you mean?" Mr. Penman asked with not a trace of anger.

He was quite open to the correction that pupil wanted to make.

"I want every one of you to be attentive as Bimbahun solves the problem," Mr. Penman said.

He then cautioned the class in a manner that sounded sarcastic, "Don't disturb him".

In less than five minutes, Bimbahun had drawn the correct diagram and quickly arrived at an answer, but Mr. Penman was quick to contest. Bimbahun insisted he was right.

Then Mr. Penman asked him to use another method to solve the problem. In five minutes, Bimbahun had come up with another answer. He then turned to his teacher and classmates and explained how he had arrived at the answer. Everyone was impressed; forcing Mr. Penman to compensate him with a prize: money for his lunch.

Tucking his wallet back into his pocket, Mr. Penman folded his hands across his chest and said to the class, "I knew he was correct but wanted him to be very sure of himself'.

That was how Bimbahun got the nickname "First of all, the diagram is wrong!" Fanta, a long time admirer of Bimbahun, then composed a song for him:

"Bimbahun, B.Sc. (Hons)
Bimbahun, M.Sc.
Bimbahun, Ph.D. in Sociology
Bimbahun, Ph.D. in Biochemistry"

There he stood in a wheelbarrow reciting a poem.

"So it is true," Fanta said to herself, trying hard to steady her legs that felt like jelly. "Bimbahun? Mad?" She struggled to believe but she had heard that he came back from the great United States of America wearing strange clothes, but she had not believed the rumours. Today, it was his parents who had directed her to the Cotton Tree when she went to enquire of him.

My own Bimbahun, mad? Fanta thought.

She pressed forward to take a closer look and she also tried to pick up what Bimbahum's audience was saying about him:

"He always recites a beautiful verse. He sits in the wheelbarrow all day and only hunger takes him away. He goes to his parents, eats something and then returns to his chosen abode. He then recites his verse and at the end of the day he stands up in his wheelbarrow and shouts, 'I will be running away too. Hurray!' before reciting his long verse:

Curiously, curiously, curiously.

He looked at the water curiously;
the mad man,
He looked at the river curiously
and said, keep on running there:
I will be coming to run too,
curiously.

Curiously, curiously, curiously.
He looked at the horizon curiously;
the mad man,
He looked at the sun curiously
and said, keep on coming out:
I will be coming out too,
curiously.

Curiously, curiously, curiously.
He looked at the tree curiously;
the mad man,
He looked at the palm tree curiously
and said, keep on standing there:
I will be coming to stand too,
curiously.

Curiously, curiously, curiously.
He looked at the bird curiously;
the mad man,

He looked at the weaverbird curiously
and said, keep on singing there:
I will be coming to sing too,
curiously.

Curiously, curiously, curiously.
He looked at the body curiously;
the mad man,
He looked at the dead woman curiously
and said, keep on shutting up:
I will be coming to shut up too,
curiously."

"How does one become mad?" Fanta wondered, thinking if there was anything she could do to help the situation. She decided she was going to get the story from his own mouth. One week passed and Fanta thought it was time she met Bimbahun. She cooked his favourite dish: *foo foo* with okra soup. That Friday, so many people had gathered around the Cotton tree to be entertained by the mad man. Just when Bimbahun shouted, "I will be running away too!" Fanta went straight up to him.

"Fanta?"

"Bimbahun?"

Bimbahun then sat in the wheelbarrow and started crying.

"Fanta! Fanta!" he shouted.

They held hands and the onlookers watched in awe.

The two friends had come a long way. If he had kept his promise and married her, they probably would have had a ten-year-old child now.

"I brought you lunch, Bim," Fanta broke the dream with her soft voice. "I don't know if this is still your favourite dish, but you and I are going to eat as we used to before you went away."

Fanta briefly looked at the crowd that was now mumbling loudly. Ignoring them, she turned to her long-lost love and asked, "Can you make room for me? I want to sit next to you. May I?" Tears streamed down her face.

"Fanta, I'm sorry," Bimbahun sobbed.

The crowd wondered what this well-dressed girl was doing with such a wretched soul.

Instead of giving her a seat in the wheelbarrow, he got down and hugged her passionately.

Then, with their feet on the ground, they both sat in the wheelbarrow.

"When did you become a wheelbarrow man?"

"The very day I returned, not quite two weeks yet."

"I was here a little over three weeks ago but didn't have the courage to come over to you. But I knew the mountain must come to Mohammed," Fanta said cheerfully.

She then put her hand on his shoulder and continued, "I have heard so many versions of your story but I want to hear it directly from you. Did you complete your school in America?"

Bimbahun sat in silence; dropped his head before he answered.

"Fanta! I used to peddle cocaine until I was caught". He had dropped the bomb.

"On my return home, my politician friend, whom I used to work for, abandoned me. My relatives disowned me too. However, my parents have been feeding me every day but they will not let me live with them..."

Fanta listened quietly not wanting to interrupt him. She only nodded from time to time.

"I sleep in this open wheelbarrow," he snorted. "I know it is unsafe but every stage of life has its own beginning. Even mosquitoes deserve their moment of celebration. Ha ha ha," he joked and laughed darkly. "They have shared their good moments with me. The world has called me a mad man and I have to be that for now until I am able to rise again."

Fanta finally interjected.

"My cousin has a spare room in the boys' quarters at the back of his house. I will talk to him tonight to see if he could take you in".

They quickly finished their food, which they had ignored when Bim was narrating his story.

"Did you enjoy your lunch?" Fanta enquired.

"Oh yes. You have just reminded me of our school days. Thanks for loving me," Bimbahun replied.

It was drizzling lightly. Even though Bimbahun's new home was at the back of another house, he had a good view of the sea. He could see the ships that berthed at the Queen Elizabeth II Quay. Through the window, a few feet beyond, he also pictured in his mind's eye the cargo they unloaded

"Why do the ships unload their cargo but never take anything away in return?" he asked himself.

Why did his friends in the cocaine ring abandon him after he was caught? Did he have any more purpose on planet earth? Does God still care? he pondered.

Fanta sat at the edge of the bed watching him while he stood by the window.

"The Americans caught me a long time ago," he said to Fanta. "I was on scholarship and the frequency with which I travelled across the Atlantic Ocean made the CIA curious and they placed my name on their list".

Fanta opened her mouth to say something but quickly shut it as Bim looked straight at her and then continued.

"Sierra Leone, Cameroon, Liberia, France and then to America. There were clergy involved in the game. So too were government officials. I always travelled with envelopes addressed to several priests in America but those were posted whenever I transited Paris."

He stopped, shook his head, closed his eyes as if reliving the moment and then continued.

"In the last two years before I was arrested, those envelopes landed on the investigation tables of the CIA. I never got to meet with any of the priests whose names appeared on the envelopes. Oh, how money makes and unmakes after intoxicating us! I did not really care as long as my occasional support got to my bank account. This too had stopped two years before my arrest but I did not know about it because I had access to lots of money from my bank accounts both in Africa and America. To add to my frustration, my Cameroonian girlfriend cut off communication with me the moment she heard of my arrest. Who wants to be associated with a drug dealer? But she was constantly feeding on its dirty proceeds."

Fanta got to learn the lyric and it became an anthem to her. She recited it before going to bed. The only difference was that she had no reason to end it with the statement, "I will be running away too!" Hand in Hand, Bim and Fanta strolled across the school football field and walked straight into their classroom; Form Four. The classrooms were all open except for the science laboratories. They both sat in their old seats. Fanta then said, "We must play the mathematics lesson once again. Today I am going to play the role of Mr. Penman. You will be the same Bimbahun. Thank God there are some broken pieces of chalk here."

The same chalkboard was there on the wall, now rough and discoloured. The tables were also rough with age though not as rough as they had expected them to be.

Fanta drew a rhombus before asking Bimbahun to rise up and solve the old problem. Bimbahun did. Fanta was shocked to see that he remembered both the question and the solution to the nearest detail. He turned, looked around as if looking at the same crowd that was watching that day and then walked carefully to Fanta. She opened her arms and they hugged. The kiss was longer and deeper than any they had ever had.

Fatu Melemeleh

It was 11:00 in the morning and the sun was already beaming broadly. It was very hot and the day was busy!

The café did not miss out on business as people came in, hurriedly ate their food and left. One could tell they were nationals of different countries by the strange languages they spoke and in the manner in which they saluted each other as they met. It was not a classy place but people loved to visit it; more so when the food was good.

Its fame was mainly due to Fatu, who had displayed her Liberian culinary skills especially with the palm butter soup that had become the favourite for many Gambians. For some reason, Fatu now sat on a big stone next to a log tethered by a chain—a very good cook turned prisoner. She sat there all day long saying nothing. When she needed the toilet, she signalled with particular signs. Her former kitchen mates would lead her, holding one end of the chain. Afterward, she trailed back to the same place and they padlocked the chain to the same log. When she first arrived, she told them her name was Fatu. But they later added 'Melemeleh', because they said she 'melted' when she spoke to men.

"Aunty Jane! Aunty Jane!" She shouted, much to the astonishment of everyone who had not heard her speak.

"What are you doing here?" the lady asked in surprise. "Why are you chained?" she continued, scanning Fatu from head to toes.

"They say I am mad so they chained me to this log, which has become my closest friend for almost a month now," Fatu said and burst into tears.

"What are you doing here?" Fatu asked wiping the tears running down her cheeks.

"You! I came here in search of you. Why did you abandon our sewing shop?"

Fatu sighed heavily.

"I came here in search of something that I don't even have a name for. At one stage, I wanted to go to America but I could not get a visa. The almighty America with its almighty dollar rejected me."

Aunty Jane walked closer to Fatu, sat next to her and wrapped her hands around her.

"Why didn't you return home?" she asked restfully. "Your shop would have made a lot of money if you had left it with me," she continued.

Fatu said nothing and for some moments the two women were quiet and only looked at the vacant sea. Aunty Jane ordered lunch and she and Fatu ate in silence. The girls at the café gossiped quietly.

"Why did you decide to get mad here?" Aunty Jane teased.

"If this had happened in Monrovia, it would have made every logical sense," she continued in a rather light-hearted manner and beckoned to the girls for the key but they pretended not to see.

"Me, mad? Gambia? Liberia? What difference does it make? Monrovia heaped insults on my head and demonized me. It was too much for me."

Aunty Jane started to say something but was abruptly stopped by Fatu's interjection.

"The most sensible thing for me to have done was to leave the country. But the Americans denied me a visa because I didn't have enough money to shower on their bars, beaches, churches, restaurants, schools, etcetera, and etcetera."

119

Breaking down again, she snorted, "No, I'm not mad! I have not lost any of the screws in my head." Her eyes were now red hot. This surprised Aunty Jane but she still did not want Fatu to notice her unhappiness. "From America where would you have headed?" she, instead, asked.

Fatu sat silent, gazing blankly into the air. Walking a short distance away, Aunty Jane looked at her straight in the eye and said: "I'm sorry to say this, but you are stupid." She put one hand on Fatu's shoulder and continued her reproach of her.

"I have been your friend and confidant for fifteen years. I sponsored you to become a successful seamstress and was prepared to see you through a degree course in clothing and textile but you said to me, in very clear language, that you were not an academic."

Fatu, shaking her head, said in a weak voice, "I know, Aunty" but she was interrupted by Aunty Jane who still wanted to continue with her reproach. "And one more thing, what happened when you visited pastor? You told me you were going to see Pastor Marcella but you never came back to say what happened."

Fatu hesitated but Aunty Jane encouraged her to explain.

She shook her head, not wanting to put her aunt to further distress, for she remembered that Aunty Jane had also gone through a traumatic ordeal; losing a grown-up son to the sea. She got up, after being freed from her shackle and walked casually toward the sea whose pristine quality the seaweeds had consumed.

The two women walked in silence. Fatu felt offended that the lapping of waves mimicked her heartbeat. In fact, what offended her more was the feeling that the sea might hear her story and repeat it to the many visitors on the beach. *Why should the world hear her story without her permission?* she thought.

"What shocked me most was when Jumu said he didn't know me. And that we attended the same church but he had never been my boyfriend," Fatu blurted. "He denied that he ever promised me marriage; a lie from the pit of hell. I lost it and fainted and only came to myself again in the hospital. I was told the pastor had taken me there and left me in the care of a doctor. Like a Good Samaritan. Imagine!" Aunty Jane paid keen attention to Fatu's ranting. She literally remembered Jumu begging her to allow her marry Fatu but felt Fatu herself was part of her trouble and she said so,

"Fatu, you have yourself to blame."

"Aunty, I'm sorry. I was just confused. Later on, I got to know that Jumu had impregnated the other girl and her parents had insisted he must marry her. Maybe you would have also fought for him to marry me but let's stop crying over spilled palm oil," Fatu ended infuriatingly.

Aunty Jane recounted the lies Jumu had told her about Fatu going to Ivory Coast to seek for greener pastures, how she even planned to go to America and how he had given Fatu $10,000.

"What!" Fatu didn't believe her ears.

"Jumu also told me that you found a new lover in your country of sojourn so he decided to marry your friend because she happened to be most sympathetic to him at the time," Aunty Jane said and sat on the broad rock just by Fatu.

Aunty Jane pleaded with Fatu to return to Monrovia, promising her a new life. "You need to face reality, my dear child."

Fatu was silent for a while. It was now 2:00 p.m. and it was very hot. Aunty Jane proposed they move to the nearby tree on the beach and sit. It was cool there. While they sat in the shade, there was an acrobatic display of some five planes over their heads. They stood up to watch like the other people on the beach were doing. The Gambia was celebrating Independence Day.

After a brief silence, Fatu continued her story. Aunty Jane wished she would stop but Fatu was passionate so she allowed her to relieve her mind.

"That's right. I didn't chop it alone. Onijibiti, my new boyfriend helped me finish it. I met him when he had just come out of jail. He was incarcerated for six months for money laundering."

"What?" Aunty Jane asked, a little confused about where the conversation was going.

"He worked as a cook in that café. The proprietress had a lot of respect for him. Of course, they both came from the same village in their country so she always protected him." Fatu went silent again. This time there were tears rolling down her eyes.

She then went on, "Onijibiti is a big thief but I couldn't even guess. I was so much in love."

"Don't say you didn't know he was a thief. The moment he introduced himself to you as a money launderer, he was telling you his name and character: Onijibiti the thief, Onijibiti the deceiver, Onijibiti the liar, Onijibiti the womanizer!" Aunty Jane burst out.

Fatu was now speaking to herself as if demented.

"My first disappointment was when he forced me to have sex. We both claimed to be born again Christians! One day, he called to say he was on a plane flying to Holland. About an hour later his girlfriend and her relatives came and threw me out of his apartment. I was working at the café when a friend called and told me they had thrown my things out on the pavement. Can you imagine? I was so angry that I splashed the hot soup on the face of a French customer. At first, I was arrested and detained. But when the French man and his spouse got to know the state of shock I was in, he ordered my release. The proprietress was not satisfied, however. She demanded my open air detention every day. And that was why you found me chained like that."

They again sat in silence. When Fatu resumed her story again, she had cheered up a little but her voice was stern.

"My world tumbled down like a pack of cards when I heard the news. Reality dawned on me like a heavy downpour of all the false promises. I became 'Melemeleh' the mad woman. Interestingly, no Liberian came to have their meal at the café since this thing happened some three weeks ago."

"Fatu," Aunty Jane called quietly, "Let's go back to Liberia. All is not lost. We will go and pick up the threads from where you left off."

Fatu still stuck to her story. The café had given her 'free' food which had sustained her until Aunty Jane had discovered her.

"I will go with you. I know that you will be there to support me all the way. Thank you! I can feel the hand of God taking the heavy jacket off my shoulders. Thank you!" Fatu found herself finally saying.

The cool sea breeze brought a piece of music Aunty Jane had not heard for a long time. It was from the café. It was now 4:00 p.m. and they needed to go. The scorching sun had cooled down. As they walked back to the café, Fatu continued her story.

"I asked Onijibiti where he got money for the trip. He told me on the phone, 'Why don't you guess? This time I out-tricked them and I have now graduated from jail for good because I now have enough money for me to never go there again,' he said. Then I asked him, 'What if you have to go to jail again?' I was surprised at his answer, 'Jail is meant for humans, not animals. I'm always prepared to go there. I'm prepared to even die there because people younger than me are dying every day. I will suggest that you think about yourself and how you will manage your life after today. Goodbye!' I can still hear his voice and the click as he hung up. His friend came to me while I was chained and whispered in my ears that Onijibiti arrived in Holland safely and was looking for a business partner. I responded with my tears only. I have spoken with my eyes only ever since. With my tears only. I still have some left in me. Tears! Yes, I said tears".

Njanguma Momodu

The Concorde

Some three hundred miles from the revs of the nearest car engine, and after half a day's trek in the shade of masasas, baobabs and irokos, I finally reached a moonworld of wonder—a world of light flies, a wolf's cry and bat's screech, where it took me some four eyes to see beyond the ordinariness of things; see the extraordinary in the ordinary.

That was the world of the Concorde—a world where I saw how the toffee brownness of a peanut shell gave way to the metallic grey of the Concorde of the night. There, where a slight of hands, gave me the third ear to hear the revving storm and the swift take off of the night craft, just like those on commercial websites, in cinemas and at the Lungi International Airport. A world where I'd been mesmerised by the trail of grey fumes in the sky just as I had once thrilled myself (in my primary school days) with my paper plane held at the tip of my fingers as I revved its engines with my puffed jaws. What an unearthly world, where the magic of touch allowed me access to see movement in stillness, hear the voice of muteness, see a cardboard flatness of things take on form and loom large like a juggernaut. There, where the lips of lips in my ears had initiated me by spluttering some arcane words, whose awesome effect had glued my eyes to an eyepiece of a night telescope with wide lenses, giving me a close-up of the most enchanted world I had ever seen. A world of faces with dark, hollowed sockets for eyes, a world where the night craft was not powered by unleaded kerosene but spells; a dark world where indecipherable words spiralled out of boiling cauldrons, where the hands of the slightest of hands, amid some serious incantation, whipped up spells of transformation. A world, tucked away in that remotest part of the African jungle, where my four eyes showed me a mysterious airport, complete with marked and lit runway, cosy restaurants and arrivals and departures lounges, manned by assistants with ruby eyes. A world where the night aircraft needed roughly an inch or so of space to land and take off.

This was how I came upon one of them...

December 1980. I was twelve when Papa finally came up with a plan, credible enough to persuade me to go to his village.

"I've got grand plans for the village, to dig out manholes, use them as toilet pits..."

According to him, they weren't going to be flush toilets like the ones we used in the city, but, at least, I would have a toilet and not have to go to the bush. I was going to be the chairman of the project, 'a life saver' as he called me, because if the people didn't use the bushes and the streams as toilets, then they wouldn't die so early of tape and hook worms.

I agreed.

A half day's trek on a laterite path in the dense jungles of Africa and under the cover of darkness dotted with night flies, the wheeze of mites and croak of frogs brought us to Peyimanday village, in Sandoh Chiefdom. Papa had a key to the front room of his house. He unlocked the door and we staggered in, dropped our bags, shuffled into our nightclothes and rolled into bed.

Early in the morning, in one eager sweep, I took in the entire village: some twenty mud brick houses with thatched rafters ringed the village square, which was a flat, sandy concourse dotted by the thatched canopy called the *Barrie* in one section of the village and a mosque in the middle of the other section. We'd lodged in the only zinc-roofed house and from its veranda I amused myself with the bleat of goats, the defensive skittering of hens with their brood, children's ditties drifting in the air and the inevitable swirling of grey smoke from the cooking cinders behind each of the houses. Every so often, the relentless pounding of pestles in mortars carried through the village, like the news of Papa's arrival.

Soon, my veranda was packed with men, women and their barefoot children. They had all come to pay respects to their industrious son from Koidu city. Meanwhile, one topless child with a large and hard stomach sat up close and whispered in my ears.

"Is it true," he said, "that the city houses are as tall as a palm tree?"

I nodded and he gasped. Then the questions tumbled out: "Are city roads made of tar?" "Do the tyres of cars and bicycles run on them?" I nodded again and as before there was a chorus of gasps. "Are there toilets in the houses?" "Is the city mosque three times the size of this village?" "Do ships carry enough food to feed one country?"

Each time I nodded, their lips dropped in wonder; perhaps it was their voices that drew an elderly man to the gathering. He was clad in brown cotton cloth, a brown cap and matching baggy trousers. Resting on his stick, he steadied his grey head and all the youngsters rallied up and sidled off the veranda. He gave me his wrinkled, grubby hand, but because he had scared my guests, I took it reluctantly.

"Bonsu," his wheezing voice coaxed me, "won't you greet me? Come on Mowiza, and greet your great uncle."

His rusty eyes held my gaze, while his mottled lips spluttered some arcane words that were beyond my age.

"I heard all the wondrous things that you've shared with the children." He coughed and his breath reeked of tobacco and kola nut. "But did you know that whatever the white witch has by day; the black wizard equally has by night? Only that ours is a great secret..."

"But Big Uncle," I said, "my pastor says wizards don't exist and we shouldn't believe in them."

At once, his eyes narrowed. The grin disappeared and was replaced with a stern look. His face dropped as he shook his grey head, as if in sadness for me. He laboured to turn and he started off. Then he suddenly stopped, half turned and said,

"So you don't believe, eh?"

I shook my head.

"I'll prove you wrong." He clicked his fingers, tapped his stick and ambled off.

In the high noon, I brought out a mat, spread it on the raised section of the veranda and sat down. Right in front of me, under the *Barrie*, Papa was playing a wooden game with seeds called *Wai* with the villagers. It was a highly animated game, the men swiping at each other, trying to cause a distraction or to annoy, causing their opponents to make a wrong move so they could take an advantage or get an opening for a kill.

"Get moving, and stop being a village layabout," one of the players chided Papa, "because this warrior is in a hurry."

"The strongest and bravest have an easy pose; if you don't believe me, then why not ask the elephant and the lion? So, my friend, be patient, for there is no virtue in hurrying yourself to your premature death," Papa chided back.

I was about to move under the *Barrie* when Big Uncle Bonsu appeared to the side of me. No words, just eye contact, and he beckoned, and the fool that I was then, I followed. How could I have been such a zombie, so impulsive, so stupidly curious and naive to have followed his lead?

At the back of the house, he rubbed some leaves in his palms and muttered some muffled but cryptic words under his breath. He ordered me to face the thicket; once again, I did as he asked. He crawled behind me; that was when I felt his grubby fingers press the squashed green leaves into the hollows of my eyes. The leaves felt warm but smelt lemony and musky. Then the most bizarre thing happened. The thicket vanished, replaced with a fourteen feet mesh-fence topped with barbed wire. On the inside of the fence, where before were clumps of masasas, now sprawled an airport the size of Koidu city. To the north, where before there was a forest of baobabs, suddenly sprang a field complete with an air control tower; to the south where before streamed a glassy brook, were now fleet of Boeing 707s, with wheeled bridges attached to them. The jungle of oaks, irokos and cotton trees had been replaced with a departure terminal lit with neon signs, blinking awnings and frantic shoppers. I turned and, truly, the village was still behind me, except that the only people visible to my dark, hollow eyes were the people of the night; for instance, the man playing against Papa had a trickle of caked black blood on his cheek. As if not to deny myself the initial wonder, I turned to the airport again. There, up close, in front of me, was the Concorde. It was grey, and had a metallic shine, with the crew toing and froing on its high steps. I saw the pilot in his white shirt with stripes and epaulets and an officer's cap. The hum of coaches and the blearing of ambulances on the tarmac had long drowned the loud bravados of the gamblers under the *Barrie*. The lights, some strange markings on the gleaming tarmac all pulled me in, but I resisted. "No," I muttered to myself, "it can't be." Of all places, an airport couldn't possibly be here, because the nearest place to see a car was half a day's journey away. I couldn't tell whether the leaves were poppy or coca leaves, but one thing was certain, they had hallucinogenic ingredients. Was this some sort of illusion? My mind had hardly proffered a solution, when I felt a tap on my shoulder. My uncle gestured toward two figures heading toward the village.

"Meet my wives," he commmanded.

I could only observe, for I seemed struck dumb and couldn't cry for help. Secretly, I prayed for this vision to end, because of the most bizarre things that I saw: the two women seemed to walk on the flat of their palms with their legs in the air. On their soles, they balanced basins of cooked rice, corn, hoes, cutlasses and other crude tools from the farm. One woman had strapped her baby to her calf, and rocked it to sleep. At this sight, my innards shrank, my stomach churned, my entire being recoiled from the hideousness that seemed to suggest that someday, I could be like these women. Held between the world of reality and the world of the night people, I felt clammy, but like a zombie, I could do nothing to help my situation. I didn't know where to start. Secretly, I wished for God's intervention, and as though he had heard me, and it was not some considerate part of my Big Uncle that had decided to relieve me, I felt the same grubby hand on my face. To my great surprise, the Concorde, the fencing, the sprawling and bustling airport had been replaced with masasas, baobabs, cotton and poplar trees.

Big Uncle edged forward and, once again, I sheepishly followed. We headed close up to the thicket and there, where four footpaths met, I saw a gleaming peanut shell. Stupidly, again, it was my curiosity that prodded me to pick it up. However, I had almost possessed it, when my uncle halted,

"Stop!"

"Why?"

"Remember what you saw, two minutes ago?"

"Yes." I straightened up and frowned.

131

"But, but it was more like an hour," I rejoined.

"Never mind." He nodded with the teacher's satisfaction of delivering a brilliant lesson.

"Did you see anything?"

"Yes Uncle, a Concorde... some concordes?"

"Very well," he said calmly.

"That was a Concorde. To the ordinary eye, it's a peanut shell, but in the eyes of the night people, it's a Concorde. Spells make the biggest difference."

Back on the veranda, heaviness lifted from me, and that was when the pestering started.

"Mowiza," said Papa, "we've just got here…"

"I know, Papa. But I miss Mama already."

"At least stay for a week, I promise..." he coaxed.

"No," I said and he knew something was not right.

The next day, my cousins accompanied me back to the fold of my mother in the city. I swore then that I would never return to the village. The fear of the caked blood on the wizards' lips had puked and driven me to the church of the *Lord Aladura* among the prayer warriors.

December 2000, at the fortieth day ceremony of my Big Uncle, I led my prayer warriors away from all the pagan elements: the masquerade, the incantation, the libations, the tympanic tom-toms, the clayed faces and the cadaverous white robes, to embark on a three day fasting and prayers. On the first day, the sprinkled, holy water became petrol or acid to the skins of the witches and wizards, and the binding powers of prayer became a bolt of fire. Before my wide eyes and drooped lips, I saw my Big Uncle's two wives (each one laden with a black pot) lead two men and two women into the village centre.

"Please please please!" they babbled and flounced as though possessed.

"Please put out the fire!" They rubbed their eyes and groped. The incense must have burnt their eyes, I thought. Our prayers soon released their grips on the black pots and they smashed on impact and spilled their contents: clipped finger nails, pieces of cloth, a badly scratched family photo in black and white, a lock of hair, a wooden doll pricked with needles and a band of red thread tied about it. I watched my great aunts grovel on the floor, writhing in pain and scratching themselves like lunatics, while the pastor sealed the prayer.

"Lord, accept these new souls." He shut his eyes; tightened and clenched his fist. "They've confessed their sins, therefore cut them loose from their oaths with the dark coven."

"Amen!"

"And accept them as new converts to your church..."

"Amen!"

By the end of the prayer, the church had won six new converts, and I couldn't wait for the second and third days of prayers.

Equainneh-Goddess of Catharsis

At dawn, the gong woke me. I sat up on the mat at the base of my shrine and submitted myself to my gods. First, I chewed on a kola nut and spat it at the bust of Nhana, spirit of divination and purification. No need to knock the gong, because the mirror on top of the bust, at the base of the Iroko tree, was already smouldering. I took a swig of the heady spirit, *Omolay*, spat it at the bust, gnashed my teeth, flexed against its spell of dizziness and started pleading,

"Eyes of the future, intercessor between us and our spirits of yonder world, your servant is listening; your wish is my command."

The smoke thickened but there was no voice or any movement, so I struck myself with the cow tail, my staff of office; a masochistic move to get my forebears' attention; then another bang on the gong and the whipping would have continued if the mirror had not clouded over. The same weedy voice gave its divination.

"That's enough, my humble servant, pain me no more with your constant whipping; we're one: your pain is mine. Spare me this morning's ablution, something urgent has come up, we have a great visitor, so get ready. Take some ashes from between the cinders in the fireplace, wrap them in cocoyam leaves, and put them in your raffia bag. Take a cowry shell and put it in your bag; at the village square, shake the shell and hold it close to your ears. I shall speak to you then, but before you go, see this...."

The smoke cleared in the mirror and was replaced with the image of a thick crowd of people teeming on the village square. They'd formed a wide ring about a banshee of a woman with a *congo-pan* of water on her head. Drenched with a mixture of sweat and water, she staggered this way and flounced that way; her eyes all upturned and egg white. Babbling, she floundered north; barking, meowing, howling like a wolf in the west.

"No brute force," said the spirit, "can free her glued hands from the pail of water. No diviner can keep her still, no tape can seal her ranting lips; none, but you... there is no time to waste, so go, go!"

I'd hardly set off, when three sweat-shone young men prostrated themselves before me in greeting on the village path leading to the open square.

"Eyes, l-l-lips, and ears of our gods," they chorused. "Chief Yabi sent us...."

"Sssssh! To release a woman from the grip of the water goddess?"

Their eyes widened as they looked in bafflement from one to the other.

"How did you know, wise one?"

"The ways of the gods are strange."

I led, and they would have followed with numerous questions but for the fact that we were already at the centre.

"Eyes of our God! Thank you for coming at such short notice, mouthpiece of the gods, we're but humans, please forgive us of any sin we might have committed and release our daughter from her burden," Chief Yabi showered me with praises.

I nodded and reached into my bag, brought out the cowry shell, shook it in my fist and held it close to my ear. The shell felt fleshy. It had transformed into lips and they started whispering.

"Take the ashes wrapped in the cocoyam leaves. Pour them in the flat of your palm and blow them in the air."

The lips then hardened, turned from pink to white and shrank. With the shell back in the bag, I did as the voice had bidden. The ashes swirled and cleared. The villagers ran in all directions of the village at the sight of a fair-faced maiden with a slender neck. She sat in the pail of water. Her lush hair dropped onto the ground, though some strands had served as glue to fasten the possessed Bandakoh's hands to the rim of the pan.

"Call them back," said the maiden, and I beckoned for the villagers to reassemble. Stealthily, they sidled back to the fold and listened to the maiden in the pail of water on top of Bandakoh's head.

"People of Kohyah," her sweet singing voice greeted them.

"I come in peace. I'm here to free three seriously sick children. I'm here because at the stream I heard the cries of three mothers, each with a sick child. I am Equainneh, the spirit of catharsis, pure heart and justice. I'm the spirit of the salmon stream, the one whose father buried her alive in a manhole lined with deer hide and wattle leaves because I exposed him as the murderer of seven maidens, whose private parts he'd used in a ritual to gain extraordinary powers and eternal life. I was buried alive, yes, but my blood was not supposed to touch the earth, but who could have known that the gnawing of the sharp teeth of mites, rats and ground pigs would be the ones to grant me my freedom beyond the wickedness of men? Hence, these agents allowed my blood to be spilled through the hide; it seeped through the soil through the pores of the earth into this stream. This stream might have other impurities like the eggs of tadpoles, algae, hook, tape and canker worms which are not spiritual, but spiritually, it is pure, as long as I guard it, and no one with blood on their hands shall fetch it and go free. Therefore, I command you,

Bandakoh, to confess right away or be burned to ashes and blown to the winds."

Suddenly, the possessed one started screaming,

"Ohohoh!" She marched and fanned the air, sweating and screaming.

"Fire, oh hot-hot fire. I will confess..."

"Ehhhhh!" a great murmur of consternation spread amongst the crowd.

"I did it." She shivered.

"I mean, we did it. Our coven is responsible for the sickness of the three children. We've already eaten several other children."

Then I pressed her,

"How?"

"Wise one, we normally use spells to fish their souls, next, we turn them into animals of our choice, butcher them and then each of us will eat our individual share."

As if they had heard enough, a band of warriors parted from the crowd. They reappeared a few minutes later in deer skin coats, cotton cloth kilts, with clay on their faces and armed with bows, arrows and machetes.

"Kill her! Kill, kill, kill!" they chanted.

The children and women ran off, as uncontrollable tears rolled from Bandakoh's eyes, but from the flowing lush hair, the water goddess raised her slender hands and the warriors halted.

"Enough of these tears," said the goddess.

"Damn your cult and your sworn oaths of secrecy. You've three days to name the other members of your cult, in front of the priest of Nhana, the chief and the elders, or you'll die," she pronounced and vanished into thin air; the pail dropped and spilled its half-emptied contents.

Ignored by all, including her husband, Bandakoh buried her face in the dust and remained sprawled on the square. I shook my head and headed back to my shrine.

The next day, in the hot afternoon, I heard some distant cries. I consulted my spirits from the far beyond. Once again, the mirror clouded and the smoked cleared and there they were. They'd ripped their wrappers and used it as strings, reinforcing them with sturdy ropes. I nodded in satisfaction with the gods, to see the witches dangling by the noose with their tongues hanging out. Like the other two witches and a wizard of their cult, all three witches twirled like puppets on strings. In the dense thicket, beside the stream of the evil forest, the crows' and vultures' circle was overhead. I nodded again.

I would have rested for the day except that in the mirror, the same three strappy young men were heading toward my shrine. So I sat up and collected some herbs and my sac for the purification of the village.

Philip Foday Yamba Thulla

Falang

I

Pa Foday sat on the edge of the wooden chair fuming. He was completely fagged out after a whole day's journey and he craved rest, but could not for the chair kept wobbling, and he had to work to keep it balanced. He never thought his father would do as he had always said, bringing them here to the village, a place they had left so long ago. Now, they had to deal with the inconvenience of the rainy season in a village! "Such a primitive man," Pa Foday mumbled. This village, Makerie, which his father had so passionately talked of as if there were none comparable to it, was just a thicket of forest surrounding a few thatched huts. His father thought children needed to know their roots, so he had eagerly sought to make this happen. Now his sons feared starvation or brutality from their relatives.

Pa Foday's elder brother, Junior, nevertheless, sat comfortably some distance away in a similar bamboo chair. He was probably equally weary, but he hardly showed discomfort even in the face of adversity. He had never objected to their father's frequent proposals of starting a farm in this village or to being sent to test the hard life here. He didn't mind being initiated into the *Poro* society and many more out of touch groups. That's why Pa Foday was angry with his brother sometimes. Junior had had nothing much to lose back in town.

"He is not the kind of guy girls will miss," Pa Foday mumbled, looking crossly at Junior sauntering about, for he was now deeply involved in the game the dirty-looking boys their uncle had introduced to them as cousins were playing a few meters away. The urge to join them pressed, but Pa Foday resisted; he was not ready for any joy just yet. The heat of anger and longing still burned inside him. He was resolute that this time—no matter what attraction presented itself—he would not be lulled by it. *Now, Papa had done it; he had succeeded in sending them to this godforsaken place*, Pa Foday thought bitterly. It was almost 6 pm, and the birds flocked as they flew to their roosts. The trees swayed in the gentle wind. Late farmers hurried to their huts, their wives trailing behind, carrying full sacks and babies strapped to their backs.

A few strong men and their children hurried by with bundles of wood on their heads. Pa Foday observed every movement but he was indifferent. Thinking again of his brother, he suddenly wanted to know what game they had been playing. The game had ended and they all were walking tiredly toward him. He could actually see the stench oozing from their bodies; they looked like coal miners. What fascinated him most was how quickly his brother had entangled himself with these cousins; looking almost like them save for his trousers, which refused to be completely tarred by the dirt.

They all moved past, some with clothes offering some covering and others, bare-skinned. As if they had been scared by some strange creature, the boys simultaneously took to their heels and raced toward Pa Foday's. He edged away as they came scrambling, almost knocking him out of the way. Pa Foday struggled to regain his balance, stealing accusing glances at the other boys and muttering something that was indistinct. The boys could see he was not happy with them, so each apologized.

"*Tank eh*," some said almost instantaneously. "*Sorü*," a few ventured in *Krio*.

Pa Foday did not reply. He just heaved himself in his seat and looked vaguely into the air. But the boys had all come to sit around him, waiting for Junior who now strolled lazily to meet them, unable to keep up.

"Pa Foday, we have to find water and wash," he commanded the moment he reached the group.

"I am not washing; I am not dirty," Pa Foday said obstinately.

"You need to. Look at all that dust," Junior said, gesturing at Pa Foday's body. Used up, he sank lazily onto the trunk by his brother's seat. The other boys just watched the interaction between the two brothers with keen interest. They giggled intermittently, especially when Pa Foday talked or fumbled about.

"Eh! Wata, wata," Junior called out to the boys making signs that indicated he wanted to bathe.

The boys looked at one another before Raka, the eldest in the group, offered an explanation to the others although he himself was not sure it was what Junior meant.

"Mant kambukor Komoryifor yeng."

The others got the joke, and they all got up simultaneously as if all they had been waiting for was that statement. Raka yanked Junior over to the side and muttered happily, *"Maskorbukor do bath."*

With the same gush of euphoria, the boys raced across the yards.

II

It took some time for Junior and his new-found friends to get to the stream. The path was rough, and they had to be especially careful not to end up in the forest that housed the *Poro Bush*. The pathways looked the same, and only a big cotton tree separated the two bushes.

"The *Poro* devil can kill anyone, even society members, who venture into the *Poro Bush* at this time; regardless of whether societal activities have resumed," Raka whispered in *Themne*.

So, the boys had to move on with a minimum of noise. The stream was a small pool that had served the villagers for about a thousand years or more. It never dried up, even in March. Perhaps, the trees that surrounded it, making it look as if it was fenced, were the reason it had withstood all weathers. The water was used for all purposes. From drinking to bathing, laundering to cooking, but at this time of the year, young men and women used the stream for frolicking. The moment the boys got to the stream, they raced into it and splashed water about, hitting the water violently with their hands. Soon, everyone was drenched and choking. Junior took his time to enter the stream, but he too was soon drenched by the splashing. The water was extraordinarily cold, and the *Harmattan* breeze bit ferociously. Junior swam on carefully feeling the cold water stinging his skin, but soon he was with the other boys splashing water into the air. They played many games until their eyes were red and watery. Around 6:30 pm, the boys started their journey back home. The big trees made the forest dark and the pathway difficult to track. As they wended their way through the dark forest, Raka explained the mystery of the stream they had just bathed in. It was called *"Bath Mishel"*, which means in *Themne* "Laughing Stream". According to him, the devil of the stream attracted people with extraordinary eyes who visited the stream and saw him (eye to eye), then laughed until they died. If Raka meant the story to scare Junior, he was disappointed, for Junior wanted everything traditional about his father's village explained to him. Back home, his father had enjoyed the respect of his comrades in the Operational Support Division of the Sierra Leone Police Force because of the potency of his *tama* (a kind of traditional protection against bullets and metals). So it became routine for Junior to come to the stream this time of the day and be enthralled by Raka's stories about their predecessors.

With a satisfied expression, Junior approached his brother, who seemed calmer now. He was sitting by Uncle Midu round a blazing fire with many other young people telling them a story. Junior and the others quickly found spaces in the circle and joined the group. Uncle Midu, sitting on a mat, feet crossed in the way Muslims would sit at prayers, was an expert storyteller. In fact, he was the village *griot*. That night, he told them stories of the brave deeds of the warriors of Makerie and of their predecessors. He told them stories of the great exploits of Chief Sama. They were breathtaking, and Uncle Midu made the telling particularly dramatic. He used songs, gestures and movements as accompaniments. Pa Foday, named after his grandfather, was glued to the action, his face smiling and almost glowing with excitement. After the stories, Uncle Midu left the gathering to have its own fun. It grew rowdy after he left, as everyone attempted to role-play the warriors in Uncle Midu's stories. Some stronger boys took the opportunity to bully the weaker ones. Then the game was changed to *Hide and Seek,* and the girls were also able to play. Often, the boys would hide, and the girls seek them out. Pa Foday reverted to his sworn self-detachment and solemn mood, taking a corner away from the maddening crowd, where he sat alone and watched. Then the game became a dramatic dance, and Pa Foday watched from a distance enthralled by the dance patterns and steps, for he too was a dancer… though not a traditional one. The drama was played as follows: girls took one end and the boys, the other end so they stood in two straight lines facing each other in even numbers. Each girl danced or walked gracefully along the rhythm of the song toward the boys.

Owe inbothr-e
De bankoroo- owo
Owe inbothr-e
De bankor
Kom de nanta mu.

She embraced the one she picked as a lover and danced away with him. Suddenly another girl, much older than the other girls, joined the dance. She clapped vigorously to the rhythm of the song in a way that quickly called everyone's attention to her. When her turn came, she danced with great dignity toward the boys who had become suddenly enthusiastic, their expectant faces stretched in broad smiles. Then suddenly, she stopped moving and moved her big buttock scintillatingly around. The clapping from the boys' end intensified, but it was noticeably dying on the girls' end. The older girl whirled round carefully as pageant competitors might do in a beauty contest, then headed in another direction and danced toward Pa Foday. The clapping noticeably slowed at the boys' end and intensified at the girls' end. Pa Foday, now totally engrossed in the drama, sat up; shocked by the sudden change of direction the girl had taken, particularly the turn it took, his way. The girl was black in complexion—jet black—but her skin seemed to shimmer and her body to glitter when the wind drove the fire, making her body seem to effervesce as she moved. Her wrap was neatly swathed around her pair of pointed breasts and brightly coloured beads were wrapped around her neck. Her hair was knotted in such a way that it curled loosely in one big, long, ponytail behind her back. She mesmerized everyone. She danced until she got to Pa Foday who she hauled up and danced with to the arena. Everyone roared. Even the boys who had ceased clapping roared and started clapping again. It was as if they had just seen Ben saving the day and rescuing Barbie from the beast in a popular Barbie fantasy movie. They both whirled around, hand in hand, for not even the most inflexible religious zealot could resist the charm of this African beauty.

III

The village was not in anyway, a sight to be proud of, especially in Pa Foday's critical eyes. Simple thatched huts were dark figures in the night. Each hut, from time to time, glimmered with a dull yellowish lamplight, and the fires, where everyone, including the dogs, warmed themselves, shone faintly in front of each one. During playtime, food was being prepared and soon, everyone was called to dinner. They rushed, briskly washed their hands and hurried to the bowls of food. Pa Foday and his brother joined the other boys and ate from the big bowl. It was like dogs eating from the same plate—there was suppressed grumbling and shoving as each boy raced to take full hands into hungry mouths. Soon, they were through eating or rather the rice was finished, and everywhere the clicking sounds of licking fingers were heard. That was all for the day and everyone rushed again to sit round the fire. This time, they sat in silence and seriously savoured the heat of the fire—the last action taken before retiring to their beds. As time went on, the clusters around the fires began to dissipate and soon everyone disappeared into their tiny huts. Inside Pa Foday's and Junior's lodge were stored all sorts of agricultural implements and locked boxes set against the wall. The bamboo bed was snugly tucked into the far corner of the mud hut; the walls dug out and stained with black from the pan lamp. The floor was scratched, gouged, and splintered. The bedspread was frayed and worn, and the mattress was as hard as a stone. Pa Foday jumped in first, then Junior, both of them slim and lanky. The smoke from the pan lamp rose in silence not far from the bed. Simultaneously, they dragged the cover sheet up and pulled it over their bodies. Junior began to snore the moment the sheet touched his skin. Pa Foday stayed awake brooding over the fireside incident. He fought to forget, but his mind was full of the anxiety as he compared the tiny physical details of his town lover—the one who had made this holiday so gruelling—to this proposed one. *Perhaps the holiday would not be as burdensome as he had imagined. Perhaps this was all just a joke*, Pa Foday thought, turning toward the wall and falling asleep.

IV

It was not a joke.

Early in the morning, just as he was about to go back to sleep to make up for staying up so late in the night, Pa Foday felt something crawling on his right leg. He dropped his hand heavily on it, but it was not a fly or some creeping thing as he had earlier thought. Fingers were scratching his legs. He held them tightly, eyes still closed, thinking they were those of his brother. It was not unusual for him to play such games. These fingers were soft and slim, however, so he was forced to open his eyes and see who they belonged to. He could not see their owner lying down, so he raised himself sluggishly up and looked down toward the foot of the bed. There she was, the lady of the previous night, standing strangely quiet. She was tall, much taller than she had appeared the previous night to Pa Foday, whose eyes now feasted on every visible part of the lady's body. She still carried on her head the woven basket, covered with a white curtain. From her waist downwards, a wrap covered her, just as it had the previous night, but her upper body was bare. Her arms were slender and there were thin patches of glossy black hair on them.

"Morning," she said in broken *Krio*.

"Good morning, and sorry I...I hit you," Pa Foday said apologetically.

She smiled, and lowering the basket, muttered, "Food." Then she emptied the basket, placing its contents on a trunk she had dragged in as a makeshift stool.

"Oh! Thank you," Pa Foday said, sitting up on the bed. "Excuse me, sorry to ask, but are you related to the Tule here?"

She gave a broad smile and her separately filed teeth sparkled. "No. My name is Ruki Kanu," she said briskly.

"Okay," Pa Foday said, feeling a little embarrassed by his enquiry.

"I should go now," she said childishly, picking up the basket and without waiting for a response, dashing out of the room. Presently, his brother and the other boys rushed in, giggling.

"What?" Pa Foday asked, looking at his brother.

"No. The food. I think God has saved us this morning," Junior said between laughs. Raka then walked carefully to the foot of the bed and said ruefully in *Themne*, "She is the envy of the village, Ruki, and she knows it, so she's conceited about it."

Soon, one of the boys rushed in hooting and hallooing that they should get ready to go to the farm. Pa Foday and the others hurriedly ate the food and got ready. The distance to the farm was dreadfully long: about eight miles on foot down a lonely path. Pa Foday walked reluctantly onward. It was strangely sunny that day. His feet were wobbling and his head was giddy, but he trod on. Finally, they reached the farm. It was big, about five acres of ground. The families tended the land in common, sharing the burden of taking care of it. Their

Uncle had gone ahead to prepare the land for the boys. All they now had to do was plant the rice seedlings. Plots were allotted, and Pa Foday and his brother were given a portion to work on. No play was allowed. When work started in earnest, everyone toiled. Plot after plot was shared till food was brought in by the women. All Pa Foday had feared happened that first day of work. At last, they walked the eight miles back to the village totally fatigued.

V

The evening was cold, but the boys went swimming in the stream. That day, Pa Foday went along, now cheerful. Junior became the guide, leading him and explaining the mystery as they went on. Raka and the other boys seldom clarified or emphasized a point. The water, as always, was ice-cold, and the boys played the same games they had played the previous evening. Junior was now familiar with most of the frolics, so was able to introduce Pa Foday to each one they played. But they were still strange games, and Pa Foday soon became confused. But slowly, he got into them. Not long afterward, they were on their way back home, and Junior told Pa Foday everything Raka had told him. Back home, Ruki had brought in the evening food and left it in the room neatly covered. The boys changed out of their work clothes, ate the food hastily and rushed to join the others round the fire where they could warm up while listening to Uncle Midu who had already settled himself in his usual spot. That night, he told them the story of the girl who followed an unknown beautiful man. Though it was a popular story, Uncle Midu's dramatic telling made it sound new to all. The digressions were particularly interesting and his version had a slight twist. The usual story told of a hero who saved the girl from a man-devil, but Uncle

Midu's version was more brutal and tragic. The girl was mercilessly swallowed by a boa.

"That's why it is not good to be obstinate," Uncle Midu ended sombrely. Getting up, he folded his mat, tucked it under his arm and walked away. There was a minute or so of silence after the story before Raka suggested a game, but the girls had spontaneously jumped into a singing and dancing session which everyone joined. Presently, Ruki appeared. When the girls saw her, they slowed the dancing and singing down, thinking she would join them, but she did not and she looked sad this night. Instead, she walked to Pa Foday, took his arm and led him away. The night was cold, but the moon was bright. She took him to a quiet place to talk. It was a small square, deathly silent—so silent; they could hear the breeze whistle. Huts were everywhere, but they were all broken. Ruki told Pa Foday it was the *"old town."*

"What do you mean by *old town*?" Pa Foday asked hastily, for they had been warned by Raka not to ever go to the old town. He was afraid but hid his fear behind a tight smile, for in the company of Ruki; he had better not take notice of evil lurking in the shadows.

"Here is where the old village used to be," she said with a broad smile, holding Pa Foday's hand and dragging him to a nearby rock he had not noticed before. There they sat and she explained all—that she had come to the square solely to seek peace, and that Pa Foday could have rest and all the air he wanted. She was weird when she spoke and often, she touched him but would not let him touch her. Often, she would edge away a bit whenever she found they had gotten too close. So, it weighed on Pa Foday not to try anything foolish. When they got back, they saw the others had gone to bed. After knocking and Junior coming out to let his brother in, Ruki said goodnight and went home alone, not allowing Pa

Foday to accompany her. Again, for half of the night, Pa Foday lay wide awake, brooding over their strange tryst coupled to an urge to have Ruki under his power, for his idea of love was, *"to get the woman under control." It slipped me tonight* he thought bitterly.

VI

In the morning, they walked to the farm and worked. Every day, the work got harder and harder, and the effects began to show in the strangers' faces—they got thinner and thinner and wearier and wearier. Ruki suddenly stopped visiting, sorrows multiplied. So, they lived entirely now on *Fofo*—day in; day out. This worried all the boys and Pa Foday in particular. "What happened to Ruki?" he asked Raka.

"Perhaps she has gone to the next village," he responded. "I will go to her place after work and find out," he continued, reading frustration in the eyes of Pa Foday.

When they came back from the farm, Raka passed by Ruki's hut to inquire about her. The others walked home and waited for him to return. He did not take long. "Ruki is seriously sick," he said, letting the sad news out. "She was wrapped from head to toe and lying in her bed," he added sadly. Pa Foday hastily got ready and went to see her. As Raka said, she was totally covered up. She was delirious and was shaking heavily, but she recognized his voice when he spoke. Pulling the sheet from her head, she spoke softly as she told him she could neither eat nor sleep. That she had seen her dead father calling out to her. Every night, Pa Foday visited her and sat by her, watching her grow thinner and thinner. She spoke less every day and her breathing was laboured. She stayed skeleton-thin, could not eat, and could not sleep. One day at the farm, the women brought the news that Ruki had died. It was no surprise to Pa Foday but he was devastated by the news anyway, and his people came round to console him.

VII

"Mo or beraka Pa Foday wufalang-e," Uncle Midu shouted, stopping his work and looking scornfully at the two brothers who were lazily planting seedlings some distance away. The other workers paused over their tasks, looking breathlessly at Uncle Midu who continued to belabour the issue. Finally, one of them enquired. *"Wu berawudeke-e?"*

"Owathfi dis-e," Uncle Midu said, smiling, his gaze still fixed on the two brothers who had been alerted by the shouting. Though completely lost, they knew the matter concerned them for the natives kept smiling, giggling, laughing and some seemed surprised.

"What?" Junior shouted back, looking at Raka, who was close by, with his twinkling eyes.

"Pa Foday's girlfriend," he said uneasily, yet with some amusement.

"What about her? She's dead," Junior reminded him.

"Yes, die but *falang*," Raka said jokingly, and the others laughed at the use of the word *"falang"* before resuming their work.

"Falang. What is that?" Pa Foday cut in.

"Somebody die and wake," Raka said with all seriousness.

"How is that possible? For somebody to die and wake?" Junior asked sarcastically, imitating the broken *Krio* of Raka.

"Yes, die and wake," Raka confirmed, moving a little closer to the two brothers and whispering in broken *Krio*, "She go visit you. She visit people and beat them in them sleep."

"Visits people? How?" The two brothers asked almost simultaneously. They were now very scared, but Junior was relentless. He thought what they had said was impossible and said so. "Once somebody is dead, that person is dead. Case closed. It is never possible for dead people to wake up again". Pa Foday watched his brother argue, but he had heard of stories of dead people who had been reincarnated. This seemed to be possible only in folktales, but he reserved the right to change his opinion given the strange behaviour displayed by his mistress the other night at the old town.

"Show me one person who died and came back to life. That people saw," Junior stammered, finding it difficult to put his thought into words.

"*Orwah!*" the workers agreed ruefully, but Pa Foday noted that it seemed to be a warning rather than a concession.

They worked in silence—he and his brother—but the natives continued to discuss the matter till the end of the day.

VIII

Back in the village, fear shrouded every hut. The firesides were quiet. Unlike normal days when the fires blazed happily and children shouted with joy, now the beautiful blaze of the fires had unwillingly dimmed, and people squeezed next to each other. Uncle Midu got to the fireside, as usual, and set the stage for his stories, telling story after story. His performances were extremely dramatic, as though he were trying to rouse his listeners from their despair and fear. But when he told the story of a man who had died a long time ago and come back to plague people, the people grew more fearful. According to him, nobody was able to stop the ghost of the man who caused terrible havoc until, one day, Pa Yamba, a powerful medicine man of the *Poro Society,* braved it to the man's grave and dug him out. In the grave, instead of finding a skeleton, he saw a skinny man still there and un-decomposed. Even his shroud was fresh and unsullied. Pa

Yamba took the corpse of the man to the village, cut him into bits and buried each one separately. "This story will come to the same ending," Uncle Midu said, ending his story and then, as usual, folding his mat and walking away. Even though many were frightened while the story was being told, the end eased them a bit, and the games resumed. That night, nothing happened, and nothing happened on the next two nights either. But on the fourth night, the complaints began again and the nights became haunted again—dogs barked and cried; goats bolted en masse as if they were being chased by some wild creature; the breeze grew violent. As early as 5 am, people came out to weep and wail. Those visited by Ruki claimed they saw her sunken eyes as she seemed to make scary faces at them, her laughter dry and cracking. Junior and Pa Foday were undisturbed, and Junior particularly slept soundly, continuing in his denial and remaining confident that people did not come to life after death.

"If goats run and dogs bark, does that mean a ghost of some sort is passing by?" he asked victims. "It is just a figment of your imagination," he said and laughed mockingly. As days went by, however, the horror intensified and many people refused to sleep in their huts. Those who did slept in groups, for it was said that the ghost of Ruki haunted lone sleepers only. But, as if becoming more ferocious, the ghost started haunting groups and waylaying farmers returning home late. These she beat back to where they came from. Junior and his brother remained free of all this, and every day, Junior fought to get the frightened villagers to be sensible.

IX

The night was foggy—the fog so thick you could hardly see through the windows. The fires could not be kept alight for long, and the huts were closed early. Outside, the trees danced reluctantly to the wind. Over the days, the sound of footsteps had become common, and this night, Junior, for the first time, felt a little frightened as the wind blew doors and windows in and out, causing them to screech. Pa Foday lay uneasily quiet, conscious of every sound and movement. The night was long, and he and his brother kept turning from one side of the bed to the other, bodies tightly covered. The door banged and they shot suddenly from the bed. Looking at each other with accusing eyes, they slowly lay back again. The wind had become increasingly violent, and even objects inside were shaking. Junior's eyes shone as bright as a cat's in the night. Pa Foday lay suspiciously still, hair standing on edge. Without a word, they both understood that the happenings of the night were extraordinary. It dawned on Junior that extraordinary things do happen, though he still doubted that a man could rise from the dead. To him, only the Bible had a record of a man dying and rising again. That message continued to give him confidence, so he called out to Pa Foday, "Pa Foday, are you still awake?"

There was no reply, so he stretched out his arm and touched his brother lightly. Pa Foday jumped from the bed suddenly, gasping. Though the weather was cold, he was sweating profusely and shaking all over. His eyes were glassy and full of tears.

"You believe these people?" Junior whispered. Pa Foday just sat still, gazing blindly into the night, still gasping loudly. "Nothing will happen," he said, hoping to coax Pa Foday back to sleep. "Go to sleep". He pushed his brother gently back down on the bed, and presently, the lamp blew out. Junior jumped up to relight it, but the door slammed, so he sat back and listened. Then, step …step …the ominous sound of footsteps was heard coming into the room. And soon after that, a bulb dangling above them, overhead, came on, casting a dull, yellowish shadow on the room. A strange creature stepped out from among the boxes. It had the shape of a man, but it was skinny and bony. It was a little taller than Ruki in real life. From the waist upward, it looked like a man, but its legs were mere bones, and it walked on stub-like appendages instead of feet. Around its bony neck hung the string of beads—just as bright as Pa Foday had seen them the other night at the fireside. The creature had a long cane stick, but the boys did not notice it at first because of the dark grey colour of its bony arms. The deathly creature gave a sudden shriek and thrust its bony arm forward, pointing the cane at the boys. Pa Foday half-fainted while Junior fought as the cane came up and down on him. After some minutes, he rolled off the bed, onto the floor, and fainted away. It happened swiftly, and then the creature pulled back the cane and half growled, half cackled, and faded away with the light. Immediately, Pa Foday roused but Junior still grunted and clawed his hands. Pa Foday rushed out, calling their uncle. Everybody was already up; they rushed to him, and he took them inside where Junior was still grunting and pointing at nothing as if demented. Instead of the natives being concerned about his state, they laughed at him. But soon, Uncle Midu came in with a concoction of herbs and smeared it on Junior. Before long, he recovered, but his pride never did. He could not say a word about what had happened. He just looked at the crowd, smiling ambivalently, from time to time.

"Don't worry," Uncle Midu consoled, "This is her last visit. Stay indoors. We are taking the *Poro* devil there now to exhume that witch," he said angrily in *Themne* and rushed out of the room.

156

It sounded good, but things were going to get much worse. Ruki had planned a much more sinister and spiteful vengeance.

Samuella J Conteh

Keep my Heart

One teary story after another spilled out of her mouth and sometimes, she gagged as her emotions got the better of her. "Why am I so unlucky in love?" she asked almost angrily. *What haven't I done for these guys? I know for sure that I am not possessed by some spirit husband that chases them away*! she thought.

The two friends always sought solace in each other's company in a friendship that slowly developed when they were transferred to work in the rural branches of their respective jobs. Their relationship had started off on official footing when they frequently met at different official functions. They had got talking and this had developed into a friendship when they discovered they both shared an appreciation for the Arts. His huge sense of humour had endeared him to her and he could just make her laugh, no matter how low her spirits were. She was particularly fond of his ability to tell a story to back up almost every statement she made. They could talk for hours and even toyed with the idea of jointly starting an Arts and Crafts business someday. There was never any question of they being anything more than just good friends—she was years older than he; he had a family. He became her confidant and she would recount the story of her love life to him. She told him how unlucky she had been in love and how, many times, her trust had been betrayed at the height of a romance. He was an avid listener and had offered support to her whenever she needed it, as she sure did that moment.

As usual, he listened till she finished her sad tale of yet another broken romance without once interrupting her. She watched his facial muscles grew tense and she imagined that in one or two instances, there was pain in his eyes. "I am sorry dear," he ventured finally. "I thought this one would be different and I noticed how much you cared for him and how happy you were with the way things were going on between you, and now I do not know what to say to you, only that I am sorry this too has ended this way". He stopped and watched the moon break through. "If you ask me, sweetheart," he continued, "you deserve better!"

But soon, she interrupted him coaxingly, "Listen, I want you to be honest with me. You are my closest friend and we have always been there for each other. You are like a favourite brother and I know you love me like a sister. You have always shown me kindness and care during my frustrations, in joyful moments and even those times when I am simply overwhelmed by the sad turns in my life. If anyone should be very frank with me, it should be you!"

Now, she was almost in tears.

"I don't want you to tell me what you think I would love to hear! Be as sincere as you can manage it, but please just tell me what you believe I am doing wrong! Tell me what I need to change about me!" she ended sadly and wiped the tears that had begun flowing from her eyes.

Well, that jolted him a bit. He muttered to himself, "There sure would be some differences in the two types of relationships—being in love with someone and just enjoying the best platonic relationship ever". She is just the same person—friendly, loving, outgoing and generous, though she could get quite crazy sometimes, but by God's grace, she deserves better than she was getting out of love, he thought.

Taking both her hands in his, he tried to soothe her nerves as he could see she was clearly overwhelmed. "We as humans are imperfect. We each have our weaknesses and also our strengths. You may have your shortcomings too but trust me; it is not your fault they leave. They are the problem! They all failed to see the real person in you. They cannot understand your strengths, your selflessness and inner values, but I tell you from the bottom of my heart, it's their loss and not yours!" he ended almost shouting.

A week later, they met at the river where they would always go to sit on the bank and race throwing pebbles. They would just be content being together and talking about any and everything. This particular evening, he could tell she was excited about something and he was sure that, before long, he would get the full account of whatever the thrill was. *Was there someone new?* he wondered. He noticed that she was taking her time letting in this particular information, so he allowed her some breathing space. They talked about many things, regular stuff like their families back in the city, who did or said what, upcoming events and the like, but nothing new. *Well, she might just be having pleasant thoughts*, he mused. They talked, giggled like school children and then she burst out, "I brought you something but now, I am not going to give it to you!" He looked at her and smiled jovially.

"Why?" he asked and he fooled around with some possible reasons to make the atmosphere light. "Did I say I was not having any of that snacks? I am, so don't let that bother you," he said jokingly. They both laughed and she pretended to hit him with her shawl. "You know that's not why and I think you are crazy," she said. Again, they joked around some silly stories he told her and then she became quiet and appeared to be in deep thoughts. The moods changed and slowly, there was tension in the air. It was like she was struggling with something that was nearing breaking point. Then, she burst out, "There is something I want to give you for safe keeping but first you have to promise to keep it well and safe. Promise you will take good care of it because it is quite fragile". "Well, well," he hesitated. This was his friend, his confidant, his crazy partner-in-crime and he knew that, though she always tried to appear tough, she relied on his support and there was almost nothing he wouldn't do for her, if only to make her happy. "You know you can trust me with anything," he continued, "Whatever that precious but fragile thing is, I promise to care for it like it were my own and my life depended on it," he ended earnestly and took a dignified position in readiness for whatever she was to give him. He waited but the silence continued and as he opened his mouth to cajole her further, she started to speak and he realized it was a story she was telling him.

Once there was a man who felt he was the luckiest man in the world. He had a beautiful wife who loved him more than anything in the world. He would brag to all who cared to listen that his was the most loving, respectful and dutiful woman for miles around. The village medicine man got to hear about his bragging and decided to prove the authenticity of the man's claim. He called the happy husband and asked him to explain to him why he thought his wife was the best. The man explained how his wife had the quietest disposition and how much she respected him and never had questioned his authority. He further explained that she was a good cook and would always keep their home clean every time he returned from work in the evening. He explained as if there was no end to the virtues of his wife. The medicine man listened with a feigned surprise and then asked the man to explain how he had been taking care of his wife and home. The man proudly explained that he promptly and sufficiently met all the needs of his wife and home. The medicine man giggled, reached into a pot by his right and took out an egg.

"Here". He opened his left hand unveiling the white sparkling egg. "Take this to your wife and ask her to keep it very well for you. Tell her that the egg represents your life and if it ever breaks, you will die," the medicine man entreated. "Do this," he continued, "and exactly a week from today, come back and tell me about your wife's attitude towards you". Carefully wrapping the egg in a white cloth, the man hurried home

162

to his loving wife. As he went, he whistled cheerfully, rest assured that this was a simple task to prove his wife's undying love for him. When he got home, he found his wife sitting on the tiny veranda of their humble home, darning his socks, while quietly humming one of her favourite local tunes. She looked up as her husband approached and she greeted him with the ever present smile that flickered her beautiful bulging eyes. He managed to keep a straight face and he invited her to follow him into their bedroom. She put down the pair of socks she was mending and immediately followed him in. When they got into the room, her husband closed the door and beckoned her to sit on the bed. In a hushed voice, he explained to her that he had been having a feeling lately that someone was trying to bewitch him, so he had paid a visit to a medicine man to get protection. He went on to explain that the medicine man had given him an egg that would represent his life and that nothing would harm him if the egg remained intact but that if it broke, he would die.

"God forbid," she cried out. "Please, my husband," she pleaded, "give the egg to me for safe keeping. You know that women are better at keeping things. You men can be so forgetful and careless sometimes". She stretched out her arms and opened her hands gingerly before her husband. "Exactly!" he said, "That is why I brought the egg to you. I know that it would be safer with you and with you, I could live till eternity," he said with all seriousness. "One more thing, sweetheart," he continued, "No other person should hear about this". "Trust me, my husband," she responded immediately, "this secret would be safe with me, for I love you more than my own life itself!" With this, she took the egg, wrapped in the white cloth, wrapped it inside another thick cloth and placed it in a safe place somewhere in her trunk. Life continued as usual between husband and wife. The husband watched his wife daily, looking for any change in her behaviour, but she remained the sweet, loving and attentive woman. The stipulated day quickly came and the husband, beaming with smiles of relief, made out for the medicine man's hut. When he got there, he found the medicine man putting some logs together but he stopped the moment he saw the man and beckoned him to sit down. "Now," he said,

rubbing his hands together and smiling mischievously, "my friend, tell me what you discovered".

"There has been no change in my wife's behaviour towards me. She is still the loving and caring wife," the husband boasted. "Have you been the same loving and caring husband you have always been?" the medicine man asked. "Do you still provide everything she needs when she needs them?" he further asked. "Yes," the man answered. "In fact, I have become more caring towards her and providing more than she needs," he continued to brag.

"Now," said the medicine man, "that is the problem! Stop being constant in your attention to her. Sometimes, give her more than she needs and at other times, give her less and at other times, nothing at all. If, after this, she is still as loving as she used to be, then it is as you have claimed, you are indeed the luckiest man alive!"

Crazy though, he thought this all sounded, he decided to see the whole exercise through. The very next day, he left just half of the usual provision for food, observing keenly his wife's reaction, but she sweetly smiled at him in understanding. Satisfied by this, the man left to do his normal business and on his return, he was met by a very sumptuous meal and he was very happy. A day or two later, he left more than he would usually do and his wife was all over him in appreciation. The husband continued the new fluctuating pattern and one day, he dared to go below the limit. When he returned home, there was no food to greet him. When he enquired from his wife, she responded in an unusually rude manner, "Go ask for food where you now take your money! What do you take me for? Do you expect me to cut off my arm to cook for you?" At this, the man lost his temper and for the very first time, slapped his wife across the face. "How dare you speak to me like that," he roared. At this, the woman became hysterical and she ranted, "You dare to slap me! Have you forgotten so soon that I hold your life in my hands? Just wait there and see what I am going to do!" With this, she rushed into the house, opened her trunk, took out the cloth wrapping the egg; her husband's life, and rushed out again. Finding a safe distance, she removed the egg from

164

its wraps and lifted it up in her right hand. "Now, this would teach you never to take a woman for granted!" Staring at her in holy wonder, he watched his wife as she raised her hand even higher, and with all her might, she dropped the egg to the ground, shouting, "Die! Bastard, die!" She closed her eyes for a moment, opened them again to find her husband walking slowly to the front of the hut, a broken man, if there ever was...

"My dear, I would not be like that woman in the story, whatever you give to me for safe keeping would always be safe. I promise to hold it very dear till you need it, God be my witness". He stopped for a moment, and then she realized they were back in real time. She looked at him straight in the eye, and with a trembling voice, she said, "My heart, can you keep it for me? No man has been as good to me as you have been. You have always treated me like a woman, a queen and that has been so refreshing. You see me at my most vulnerable moments and you have never, once, tried to take advantage of that. You understand that I get weak sometimes and just need a shoulder to hold on to and this you have unreservedly offered to me. You have shown me selfless love and in all this time, we have been friends, we have never, for once, fought, no matter how much we disagree. I am tired of trying and failing in matters of the heart, so today, I give the whole of my heart to you, to be kept away from pain, keep my heart!"

Meet the Contributors

Bakar Mansaray is a Sierra Leonean – Canadian author. In 2016, he published a book of short stories entitled *A Suitcase Full of Dried Fish and other stories*. His works have appeared in Maple Tree Literary Supplement, Ayebia African and Caribbean Publishing Specialists, Edmonton's 'Diversity' magazine, Vancouver's 'Patriotic Vanguard', and 'Christian Monthly Library (West Africa)'. He was a nominee for the 2016 Writer-of-the-year Afro-Canadian Heroes Award, and founder of the Mandingo Scrolls Series. He currently lives in Canada. His blog address is:
www.mandingoscrolls.blogspot.com

Celia Thompson is a journalist and media practitioner. She currently co-hosts the 'Day Break West Africa' breakfast show on West Africa Democracy radio in Dakar, Senegal. Lived and worked in Sudan and South Sudan, respectively, between 2007 and 2014; served as a Peacekeeper for the UN Peace Keeping missions (UNMIS & UNMISS) and then as Programs Head (Radio Miraya)—Foundation Hirondelle—a Swiss Non-governmental media outfit. Prior to that, Ms Thompson worked for the UN Mission in Sierra Leone during the post-conflict era—facilitating the Voice of Children project, with over 200 children including ex-combatants and war orphans. She holds a Bachelor of Arts degree with Honours in Linguistics, together with International diplomas in Advertising, Media Studies and Modern Management, from the Cambridge International College. Ms Thompson is a Rotarian.

Fatou Taqi (nee Cole) is an academic, an activist, an advocate and an entrepreneur. She is passionate about the empowerment of women and girls and she strongly believes that learning and education are key 'changers' of any situation. She is president of the 50/50 Group and she is Director of Academic & Career Advisory & Counselling Services (ACACS) at the University of Sierra Leone, The Students Complaints Commission and she is the ICT Co-ordinator of the University. She is a lecturer in the Department of Language Studies and the Institute for Gender Research & Documentation (INGRADOC) at Fourah Bay College, University of Sierra Leone. She is a mother of three.

Gbanabom Hallowell is a poet, novelist and journalist, and founder of the Salone Writers Forum, a WhatsApp group of Sierra Leonean writers. He has published nine volumes of poems, a novel and a diary of the Sierra Leone Civil war. His most recent collection of poems is *Anatomy of Love*. Hallowell is the editor of *Leoneanthology: Contemporary Short Stories and Poems from Sierra Leone* and of *In the Belly of the Lion: An Anthology of New Sierra Leonean Short Stories*. He holds a PhD in Interdisciplinary Studies in the Social Sciences from Union Institute & University, USA, an MFA in Creative Writing and Literature from Vermont College, USA, an Executive Education from Harvard University, and a HTC from Milton Margai Teachers College. He has taught in colleges and universities in Sierra Leone and in the United States, and is currently Director-General, Sierra Leone Broadcasting Corporation.

Harriet Yeanoh Jones is a lecturer at the Institute of Languages and Cultural Studies (INSLACS) Njala University, Sierra Leone. She holds a Bachelor of Arts degree (French and Linguistics) from Fourah Bay College, University of Sierra Leone and a Master of Arts in Descriptive and Applied Linguistics from Njala University.

James Bernard Taylor works in Project Management after graduate studies at the University of Maryland (UMUC), USA. Prior to that, Taylor worked for the US Department of State for twenty-three years as Director, Information Resource Centre at the US Embassy in Freetown. He also taught at the Methodist Girls High School and the Institute of Public Administration and Management (IPAM), University of Sierra Leone (Social Work Program). He is a published writer and poet with some of his works found in *Songs that Pour the Heart: Poems from Sierra Leone; Leoneanthology: Contemporary short stories and poems from Sierra Leone, and The Price and Other Stories.* He has also written many non-fictional pieces on socio-political issues in several newspapers. In addition to writing, James has a passion for classical music and photography. He plays musical instruments which includes the piano/organ, accordion, guitar and euphonium and has composed classical and gospel music for choral performances.

Jedidah Adlyn Olayinka Johnson is a fifth year Medical Student at the College of Medicine and Allied Health Sciences, University of Sierra Leone. Her interests are writing and medicine. She attended the Eastern Polytechnic Junior Secondary School, Kenema and the Beacon High School in Freetown where she was the head girl in 2010. She is the author of the novel, *Youthful Yearnings* published by Sierra Leone Writers' Series in 2015. She has also won a number of laurels which include: Best BECE Result in the Eastern province and Second Best in the Country, 2007; Degloma USA, Award for Excellence- 2007; Second Best Debater in the Secondary Schools Category, British Council, 2008; Second Best Debater in Sierra Leone for Tertiary Institutions-2012; Winner, National Writing Competition-2016. She is also joint winner, SLWS 2016 Best Author for going the extra mile to promote her book.

Joan Adama Kainessie was born on the 29th December, 1986 in Mattru Jong. She holds a Bsc (Hons) degree in Computer Science from Njala University. Her main hobbies are reading, writing, dressmaking and drawing. She began to nurture her interest in writing since she was in the primary school and she has been passionate to water it further. Her writings are full of lyrical 'outpourings', expressing her deeply religious, loving and mystical passion.

Mohamed Gibril Sesay grew up in Crojimmy, Eastern Freetown. He was educated at Fourah Bay College, University of Sierra Leone. His creative works include a novel, *This Side of Nothingness*, a Caine Prize nominated short story, "Halfman and the Curse of the Ancient Buttocks" included in the anthology, *"Work in Progress and Other Stories"* Published by Caine Prize (2009). Another short story, "Monkey Teeth" was published in *Focus on Africa Magazine* October-December, 1999. Sesay has had several of his poems published in local and international publications. He has lectured Sociology, worked as a journalist and served as a consultant for various national and international organizations.

Mohamed Sheriff writes children stories, short stories, novellas and drama for radio TV and stage. He produces and directs documentary videos, short films, radio, TV and stage plays for both entertainment and social change projects. He has won several local and international awards for his productions and writings including Best Short Film, "Victims", We Own TV National Film Festival 2012, Best Docudrama Film, "Sombodi Ep Mi", Sierra International

Film Festival 2 (SLIFF2) 2013 and three BBC playwriting and many short story awards (*Just Me and Mama, Spots of a Leopard,* and *A Voice in Hell*) and the ECOWAS Prize for Excellence in Literature for "Secret Fear", a novella for teenagers, published by Macmillan Publishers.

Moses Kainwo was born in Sierra Leone in 1955. He is a Pastor of the Methodist Church and is married with two daughters. He worked with a couple of NGOs before joining the University of Sierra Leone as Deputy Registrar. Presently, he is working with the Angels Global Initiative (AGI) as General Manager. His poems have been anthologised severally and his collection of poems, *Ayo Ayo Ayo and other Love Songs* is available on Amazon. He claims to owe his writing knowledge to *Falui Poetry Society* where he served as President for several years. Lately, he has fallen in love with the art of storytelling.

Njanguma Momodu was born in 1968 at Bumii (Tongo-Air fields) in the Eastern province of Sierra Leone, West Africa. The word 'Njanguma' means a big, sleek cat with 49 lives. His entire being is made up of hard-work from his late father; storytelling from his mother and his sociability and shrewd observation of characters from his nineteen cousins that he grew up with. In 1976, he went to the Roman Catholic Primary School, and in 1983 entered KSS (Koidu Secondary School). In 1988, he went to London and enrolled at the Kilburn Polytechnic, where he pursued a series of courses in business, law and economics. In 2000, he enrolled at the University of Westminster, UK and graduated four years later with an honours degree in Business Studies. Shortly afterwards, he undertook a post-graduate degree at the Institute of Education at the University of London. It was while studying at these various institutions that he started writing poems, short stories and novels. 'M'frique' was published in 'On the Threshold of a Dream' and 'Roots' was published in 'The Best Poems of 1995' both published by the North American Library. Five of his religious poems were published by Feather Books Publication and 'Bless You O Tireless Hand' was published by Still Life. Other Publications include: 2012, *The Five Fingers: fantastic fables* published by Author House U.S.A; 2015, *Daughter of Albino* published by New Generation Publisher Current projects; *Yellow Woman*–a novel *The Resin Touch*–Poetry Anthology. In addition to his work as a Business lecturer at Kensington and Chelsea College and an 11+ English Prep Tutor at Queensbury School of Education, Njanguma runs his own Tuition Centre: *Tailored Tuition* at Rayners Lane in London.www.mrmostailoredtuition.com.

Philip Foday Yamba Thulla was born in Lunsar, Sierra Leone. He holds a master's degree from Njala University in Sierra Leone. He has published a compilation of short stories, *Homecoming: Knowing My People and Other Stories* and co-authored a short novel entitled *The Chameleon Goes Home*. He is presently a PhD student in African Folk Literature (The Temne People) and a lecturer in Literature at the Institute of Languages and Cultural Studies, Njala University, Sierra Leone. He has just completed a full-length fictional memoir entitled, *Saving the State House: the Confession of a Thug.*

Samuella Julia Conteh loved reading from a very young age, and she grew up to be fascinated with books by Enid Blyton, Mills & Boon and by mid-secondary school; she could hold serious conversations on works by James Hadley Chase and others of the same genre. As she would explain, she gets transported to distant places and believes she is actually in the plots of the books she reads. With good writing skills and an easy understanding of the English Language, she ventured into writing essays, poems, prose and contemporary articles, many of which got published in local newspapers. She won a scholarship to do a distance course in Specialist Writing with the Writers Bureau, London. Samuella studied Human Resource Management and has for the past thirty years worked in several units of Office Management. She is currently with the National Human Rights Commission. She lives in Freetown, Sierra Leone with her daughter and granddaughter.

A Reader's Perspective of the Stories

Abdulai Walon-Jalloh
Author of
Voices & Passions – Poems (SLWS 2015)
Hungry Vultures – A Play (SLWS 2016)

The story, **Running the Kilmanjaro**, reminds us of the unyielding pressures of winning at all cost. The narrative paints a picture of selfishness on the one hand and on the other hand unrelenting devotion to true friendship as demonstrated by both Lenana when he slowed down so that Steve could catch up with him and when he also saved Steve from the blue monkeys though Steve had to run away quickly to take advantage when Lenana slowed down to battle a tick that was troubling him. The race to finish first in **Running the Kilmanjaro** takes centre stage. Steve and Lenana are troubled by poverty and twin love. The two protagonists must disengage from their worries to focus on the present which happens to be the race. For Steve, winning represents twin release from firstly dethroning Lenana who is the record holder and redeeming the memory of a lost friend Gaston Leduc. The mountain Kilimanjaro is brought to life in all its splendour and majestic beauty. Again, its fiendish nature is also brought home because we know that the Kilimanjaro possesses the ability to haunt its trekkers or runners with fluctuating weather and altitude sickness not to mention the attacks from wild animals.

In **My Brother's Confession,** Celia Thompson has endeavoured to portray a house of shame in all its splendour and bitterness. Fancy the protagonist and her brother King are up against a somewhat faceless adversary who is so ruthless and methodical. King, as the name implies, is majestic for the wrong reasons because cowardice and narrow-minded vision have prevented him from saving himself and his sister, Fancy from rape. In spite of the seeming wise-up antics of King and Fancy, we are appalled by their sheer naivety and meekness with which they offer themselves to Man. And Man has not been punished as far as the story goes but there is a vague wish by Fancy to have the rebels punish him by burning his red house to the ground. Celia has been able to portray a character in the person of Man who is almost faceless and nameless though he comes across as a banker with relatives abroad. The latter, a quality which is the icing on the cake for most tales today, will not endear him to the heart of the reader. The story reminds the reader of the stark realities and choices facing our young girls today. Ras, the reader might be tempted to conclude, is the issue of Fancy's rape. No wonder Fancy is always reminded about that sad day.

A Complex Situation by Fatou Taqi tells the story of Alpha, a young but excessive character who goes berserk with his trousers and drunkenness and ends up contracting the HIV from a fourteen year old virgin, Sally whom he raped viciously. Namsy, the younger sister of Alpha, represents the voice of reason and common sense which is normally unheeded whereas the School for Rogues is synonymous with everything that is wrong in that society. Sally, the fourteen year old virgin becomes a victim by nature and chance. The story, though short, is very straight forward and racy. The episodes and plots are mono-focal and unitary. Alpha and Namsy are first generation educated elites but the two are reacting differently to their newly-found status. Namsy is quite the opposite of her brother though the reader would have loved to see her character developed further as Alpha braces himself for the complex situation whereby he, an HIV positive, will marry and raise children and live happily ever after. The piece dwells on the age-old problem of good versus evil and the triumph of the former over the latter.

A Place to Die by Gbanabom Hallowell is a narrative that blends historical authenticity with fiction. The story focuses on the life of celebrated Sierra Leonean slave Joseph Cinque popularly known as Sengbe Pieh, now over eighty years old. The story is based on Sengbe's long search for his lost family. Sengbe is able to free himself and colleagues from the Amistad, later on argues their way to freedom in an American court, and returns to Africa to build a church yet he is unable to find his long lost family left behind when he was captured and sold into slavery. The piece is touching and the longing exhibited by Sengbe, very painful. In fact, Sengbe has come to die in the church but before that he must see his family (wife and children). The writer is able to present levels of contrast to inflate and deflate the persona of Joseph Cinque. Joseph or Sengbe can fight Spanish enslavers and commandeer the Amistad and his story infuses gallantry into the young African American Pastor, Pen but Sengbe's own countrymen can hardly recognise the hero in him not to talk about offering him food and shelter when needed.

Kadiatu by Harriet Yeanoh Jones is a somewhat neutral piece that wavers between two extremes in the age-old culture clash between modernity and traditional African rural village life. Kadiatu, the protagonist, develops gradually and her awareness of who she is dominates the entire plot. Harriet is a storyteller and like many storytellers, she sometimes resorts more to telling than showing. The piece is like a fairytale that ends well and everyone is happy and satisfied. Uncle Alie is so affable and the parents in the village are so considerate. The heads of Kadiatu's new home are tolerant though little is said of the father. Readers will find themselves in familiar territory wherein modernity and city life take over village life (just like travelling overseas in other stories has served as an escape route to greatness and fulfillment even if it is for the short time). **Kadiatu** is sectioned unusually but fittingly and I think this will sit well with younger readers. Harriet litters her piece with usual suspects that normally pass for success in everyday life. Take for instance the need to study, pass public examinations and delay initiation into the bondo society till the age of 18 and above. The piece, in my estimation, is not meant to hurt or belittle any side.

Falling Leaves by James Bernard Taylor is centered on sibling rivalry between Adeline and Fatu. However, most of the story is narrated by Pa Cole, an octogenarian who happens to be the uncle of Mr. Johnson, the guardian of Fatu and father of Adeline. Fatu is taken in by the Johnsons from Morlai and his estranged wife, Ya Alimamy. Sadly, Morlai is struck by lung cancer and is on the verge of dying. Fatu and Adeline are growing up well with the quality support of Mrs. Johnson, the teacher, but jealousy and mischief have caused the siblings to go apart and Mrs. Johnson has naturally sided with her daughter, Adeline over Fatu. Adeline has spat into the food whilst Fatu is not looking but she is caught in the act and the quarrel puts them apart. The reader is appalled by the response of Mrs. Johnson whose magnanimity before now has been very imposing. James B. Taylor divides the story between the Johnsons and Brer Mello whose trying circumstances have not deterred him from making it to the top though modestly. Brer Mello brings the two strands of the narratives together. Fatu is rescued by Brer Mello and after Mr. Johnson passes away and his wife, the teacher, and their daughter have fallen into bad times, Adeline is left with little option but to seek help from Brer Mello, the godfather of Congo Town Grassfield.

Letter to My Beloved by Jedidah Johnson is a truly romance piece that chronicles the love between Momoh and Egertina in Kenema, Eastern Sierra Leone. We see a determined pair of lovebirds with dissimilar backgrounds in terms of social standing defying the odds to come together at the beginning. Momoh's mother is the maid to Egertina's family headed by Dr. George. The fortunate twist to the story is when dutiful Momoh decides to go on an errand for his mother i.e. to carry a bag of coal to a neighbour where Momoh sees Egertina whom he describes as an angel (reminds the reader of Peter Parker to Mary Jane in 'Spider Man' the movie) because of her beauty and Momoh is described by Egertina as filthy though she does not mean any harm. Momoh's mother advises his son to stay away from Egertina but Momoh has been struck by the arrow of love and he is blinded by true love. By the time Egertina is nineteen and Momoh twenty-one, a Mr. Peacock has entered the scene to ask for the hand of Egertina in marriage. The father of Egertina, Dr. George does not want his daughter to associate with Momoh whom he considers as a gold digger. In fact, Dr. George will slap both Momoh and his mother in full view of the public and this is the straw that breaks the camel's back. The reader is amazed by the steadiness of character Egertina displays. She runs away and refuses to be married off like a parcel and remains single not necessarily to wait for Momoh who by such time has won the DV Lottery to the USA by which token he has become successful and has invested in his hometown by putting up a grand hospital to serve his community and the twist in the tale is set to unravel from here.

Submission by Joan Adama Kainessie epitomises what is typical of traditional African households. There is always a submissive woman so that the children will be blessed. Jatu falls into the mould of the Nyakibi in Ngugi's 'Weep not Child', Tess in Hardy's 'Tess of d'Urbervilles, Nwoye's mother in Achebe's 'Things Fall Apart' though she is unlike Wanja in Ngugi's 'Petals of Blood'. Jatu is so submissive and she readily quotes the scriptures to support her passivity for which the reader might be appalled at; as if the world is ganging up on her. 'Papa', who is nameless, is hardly mindful of the sacrifices of his wife, Jatu and Ada, the eldest daughter has long taken notice. However, Jatu calms Ada and assures her that one day she will understand. Jatu is the stoic and the backbone of the household and we see this made manifest when she passes away; her husband is never the same. Papa is humbled by Jatu's passing and the blind machismo that has dominated his life and even blinded him to the shade his wife provided emasculates Papa completely because his better half is gone. The household crumbles. Ada is no longer in school and Marie's hand is timely given to Alpha for marriage. In fact, it is Alpha who rescues the family as he takes everyone to the city after their wedding.

Chronicle of a Birth Foretold by Mohamed Gibril Sesay focuses on the labour pains of Maseray. The unborn child is being delayed by some dark forces. Maseray's husband KothYaro, Lamin's brother of the same mother and their mother are at the hospital displaying different reactions to the delayed delivery of Maseray's child. The mother-in-law believes that her daughter in law is crooked and has refused to stop bathing at night without charcoal in her bathing water and now she is paying the price of being depraved and stubborn. KothYaro believes otherwise. Gibril Sesay is lacing the drama with religion, superstition and folklore and these, more than anything else, are impressing a true sense of Sierra 'Leoneanness' on the mind of the reader. There is also the small issue of bribery and double-layered narration and the latter enables the writer to subtly intrude into the events of the unfolding drama. The things which Maseray is said to engage in are so many, thus warranting the need for her to be punished.

Sori Clever by Mohamed Sheriff is a hilarious piece that dwells on the exploits of Sori, the drunkard. Quite a brainy fellow who can always manage to make friends and enemies part with a pint or two of beer in his favour. Sheriff is able to infuse into this humorous piece issues of unexplained wealth, bribery and institutionalized corruption at the International Port where Sori was working. It is a heavy piece but dealt with lightly with the help of the comicality that is Sori Clever. Sori's inability to remain sober and win a wife, Musu, mirrors the wider societal challenge of not being able to resist the amorous advances of corruption. In the midst of this barrage of corruption, there is the lone voice of the narrator's father. Musu, the widow and her children are symbolic; representatives of where mostly the proceeds from sleaze will disappear. Sori is Musu's insurance. After the clean-up at the International Port, Sori becomes collateral damage who goes down with his Boss who, in turn, as rumoured, has fallen apart with his Boss at State House. The lack of clarity as to the exact reason for the fall-out is typical of societies in mendicant nations. Sheriff has been able to infuse another layer to this piece i.e. religious zeal or militarism as evidenced by the bold preacher who dares to preach the word to customers at the Red Hot Spot.

A Diary in the Head of a Street Child Beggar by Mohamed Sheriff shines the light on a ten year old displaced boy who is a beggar living with his grandma. It is 2 pm and he has not eaten anything since morning and this hunger is making him dizzy. In addition to his hunger and inability to attract alms from the people, he is suffering from slight coughs. His grandma is sick with tuberculosis. Before now, the boy has been living in the provinces but rebels invaded their hometown making them watch their entire family burn alive inside their house. Grandma is very upbeat and praises the effort of ECOMOG and UNAMSIL and she believes that every Nigerian soldier will go to heaven. The bearded rebel, according to grandma, is recalcitrant and has refused every offer made to him. The piece is so touching as we empathize with the ten year old who longs for heaven to be able to access milk and honey. The desire to die is worrying because the impression the reader gets is that the situation is hopeless and physically exacting on the boy. The moving piece depicts a boy who is unable to see clearly even when it is daylight. He faints from hunger and disease and society stands and looks disinterested.

Wheelbarrow Man by Moses Kainwo is a light-hearted adventure detailing the life of Bimbahun; his rise, fall and redemption. The central character who happens to be a mathematics champion at a tender age is able to correct his mathematics teacher in full view of his colleague pupils and the teacher, Mr. Penman, allows it to go on. Quite a culture shock because most teachers in some parts of the world where teachers are demi gods will never allow a pupil to correct them. Kainwo is able to orchestrate the redemption of Bimbahun who has fallen into hard times and is mad after his sojourns in the United States by creating a very fantastic character, Fanta to come to Bimbahun's rescue. At the beginning of the story, it appears as if Fanta is narrating the story but then the narrative veers off into the third person or omniscient narrator who seems to be everywhere. Kainwo's piece is a splendid tale of genius prowess, fame, humiliation, redemption and normalcy—all in support of the central character, Bimbahun. We are amazed at Fanta's boldness and faithfulness.

Fatu Melemeleh by Moses Kainwo is another classic redemption and wholesomeness tale just like 'Wheelbarrow Man' by the same author. Fatu of the 'palm butter soup' fame is making it big in a Gambian restaurant when disaster struck. Kainwo is a skilful story teller who does not delay the plots and sequences. We know the reason for Fatu being chained to a log because, after receiving the shocking news about her boyfriend, Onijibiti's betrayal, she is unable to control herself. She throws hot soup into the face of a French customer. Again, Kainwo is able to prove that solutions are not out there or in America all the time but those local home-grown solutions can be efficacious. What Kainwo is driving home is that sometimes the young should listen to reason and experience and learn to appreciate what they have instead of rushing into mirages of disappointment as a result of the hunger for the seeming glitter in foreign lands. Fatu travels to Gambia and is unable to secure a travel visa to the US but manages to keep her life together working in a restaurant. But she overreacts and has herself to blame. Fatu appears like a victim who is hurrying from one persecution to the other.

The Concorde by Njanguma Momodu is one those pieces that celebrate the triumphs of western religion over African traditional mysticism easily dismissed as witchcraft and black magic. Uncle Bonsu is able to open the young eyes of Mowiza to the power that is African traditional religion by showing him a vision of an airport replete with Concordes and other airplanes when he rubs some leaves to his eyes with the help of some incantation. Mowiza is able to see that in the other Africanworld women could walk upside-down with their babies tied to the ankles and food placed conveniently on the soles of their feet using their palms to walk. After this mesmerizing spectacle, Mowiza decides to cut short his trip so that he can be with his mother in spite of the pleas from his father. Mowiza, the narrator, will have to return to his village once more, this time for the fortieth day ceremony of Big Uncle Bonsu. And he, Mowiza, is ready as he is with his prayer warriors who are praying fervently to the Christian God.

Equainneh-Goddess of Catharsis is another fantastic achievement of colour, magic and dazzling narration by Njanguma Momodu. The Chief Priest is without a name and sex. And things reveal themselves clearly in the mirror at Nhana's shrine. There are lots of details in terms of powers and controls and delegations. The 'Banshee' is similar to the

Irish water spirit and one wonders what it is doing in Africa. The Banshee is making Bandakoh reveal her hideous secret about how they are eating three children through witchcraft. The Banshee herself is a victim of ritual murder who has exposed her father's dastardly act in order to achieve supernatural powers. The Banshee is killed ritually and her blood should not have touched the ground but with the help of 'mites' and 'ground pigs' that are eating into her body the blood touched the ground thus making the Banshee powerful and an exposer of hidden secrets. The chief priest of Nhana is the medium through which secrets are revealed even before the villagers come to consult the shrine. In this piece, Njanguma reveals the power of African traditional magic and its layered mediums.

Falang puts Philip Foday Yamba Thulla into the category of Sierra Leonean writers (which include Gbanabom Hallowell, Gibril Sesay and Njanguma Momodu) who are deploying the rich cultural arsenal of Sierra Leone into their stories in order to add colour and spice for an enhanced Sierra Leoneanness. The story is a traditional masterpiece on Themne culture and folklore. The story revolves around Pa Foday, Junior and Ruki in a village in the heart of Themne Land. Yamba Thulla enthrals the reader with Themne folk dances, songs and beliefs against the backdrop of the powerful Poro Society. Pa Foday and his elder brother, Junior have been thrust into the home of their father who had wanted his children to taste life in rural Sierra Leone. Reluctantly, they arrive at the village and are greeted and welcomed by everyone including Uncle Midu and their several cousins. During one of those traditional song and dance sessions, Ruki, the village belle, takes a particular liking to Pa Foday. In their sojourns, the two visit the forbidden Old Town and have enjoyed peace together. After that night's visit, Ruki falls ill and dies but her spirit refuses to rest in her grave.

Keep my Heart by Samuella J Conteh is an elusive piece that does not mention the names of the two to-be lovebirds. Samuella, however, cleverly presents a persona who is hungering for true love. The persona, nevertheless, has a confidant who happens to be her colleague at work with whom she shares her thoughts and vulnerabilities. The male confidant has a family but whether he is truly devoted to his family has not been made clear in the story. The story is told in the third person which gives the writer the opportunity to be objective and able to be everywhere if she so chooses. There is another story within the story in which the female protagonist narrates to her male confidant about a loving wife's dutifulness to her husband and the husband's bragging about this everywhere. One day, a medicine man hears about this perfect couple and decides to challenge the boasting husband.